By

Jim Musgrave

Published by EMRE Publishing, LLC

San Diego, CA

ISBN-13: 978-1943457182

DEDICATION

To George Orwell, who inspired this novel, and to all the veterans of militaries everywhere. I hope you soon lose your jobs. Also, to my wife, Ellen, who now has Lewy Body Dementia, and who has believed in my genius even when I didn't believe in myself.

Interactive and Multimedia Enhanced eBooks

EMRE Publishing is now selling completely "enhanced" versions of its books through the unique Embellisher Multimedia Stream platform. Simply register inside the eReader to have access to the variety of titles. They contain relevant historical videos, music, interactive content, and a complete audiobook edition in many of the great titles.

Visit https://emrepublishing.com/new_embellisher-ereader/ to see what's available. In addition, if you are also an author or one who sells online, you may want to take Professor Musgrave's free online course, "Developing Your Digital Marketing Platform" (https://payhip.com/b/j3Xs). Besides eBooks, you will learn how to sell other tangible goods and services, as well as digital podcasts, courses, and a variety of video products.

Contents

ACKNOWLEDGMENTS

I want to acknowledge the scientists and engineers at the California Institute of Technology and Jet Propulsion Laboratory, where I learned that being a realist is not the same as being a pessimist. I also want to thank all the authors of speculative and science fiction work. The inspirations they have, come from projecting into the future what is embedded in the present day. Just as all of our civil rights have been eroded, drip by drip, without the younger generation really being aware of it, we must also acknowledge the fact that genius exists far beyond the planet Earth. If we don't learn our lessons, then there will come a day when we are taught the truth on a far different level.

Part 1

Chapter One

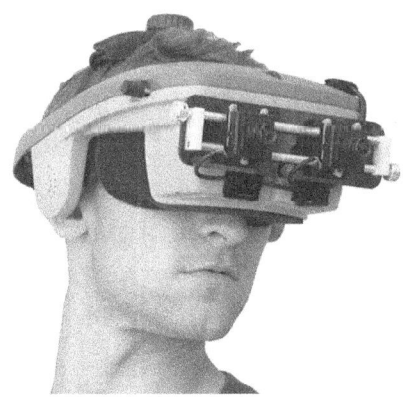

The day was again overcast. The marine layer hovered over William as he rode the YST wagon to the heart of the tourist district in Old Town, San Diego. His fellow passengers had their noses in their video screen visors that covered their faces like helmets from the Middle Ages. "Knights in white satin," William whispered to himself from a lyric he was hearing on the audio channels coming from the buds inside his ears. He preferred audio over video because it gave him a background soundtrack for his seditious thoughts. He was also able to see his brothers and sisters with much more clarity. William was turning 40 in three days, and he knew what was in store for him, but unlike all of these other digital monkeys, he didn't trust a single word that came from Big Bro's mouth.

Inside his Youth Socialist Hostel on Congress Street, it smelled of boiled ramen and yoga mats. At one end of the ranch-style building, at the end of the hallway, a huge hologram vibrated in 16,777,216 bytes of color. It was the gargantuan portrait of a man of about twenty-five, with a blond beard and ruggedly handsome features. William headed for his cubicle domicile four doors down the hall. The rest of the building was dark, as it was part of the "Put Nature First" drive to limit energy use. *Of course, that didn't prevent the infrared spy cameras from being used in every building, in every city around the world*, William thought, limping inside his sparse apartment. His soccer knee was acting up again, and he took some pride at having injured himself playing one of the banned sports. On each wall of every apartment, the same hologram gazed at you, and the eyes followed you as you moved about. The voice from the poster rang out, and it could never be switched-off to save energy or to prevent global weather changes. BIG BRO IS MINDFUL OF YOU, the voice said, in a deep bass vibrato.

Behind his simple cot and clothes dresser, the wall display was broadcasting the party's 24-hour news. It was showing the latest in digital gadgets from the party headquarters in downtown San Diego and how "mindful brothers and sisters were using the entertainment visors and meditation videos of Big Bro to reach new heights of sensory bliss." *Unless you've reached 40. Then, bliss might as well be taking a piss off Big Bro's nose*, William thought, remembering the gigantic statue of their beloved leader out in Balboa Park, next to the old statue of El Cid on horseback. William watched his own reflection in the monitor. He was a thin brother with a curly-black goatee and black racial features. Wide, flat nose with flaring nostrils, full pink lips and pink palms reflected back at him in the mirror image. William's mother, Rose, who had Lewy Body Dementia, thought that mirrors led to another world. Just like *Alice in Wonderland*. "There are no races or categories of discrimination," William smiled and spoke out loud to the spy monitor from Big Bro's propaganda. *We only discriminate against you as you get older*, he thought. "Forty is the new twenty," he spoke at the screen. *Forty puts you on automatic Anomic Suicide watch*, he thought.

Outside, the world looked cold. In the best equatorial spot on the Earth, the temperatures hadn't reached 80 degrees in over ten years. Devil winds were swirling tourist trash into spirals in front of William as he walked toward his place of employment. These were the microcosmic versions of the giant tornadoes, hurricanes and tsunamis that kept the world on guard throughout the year. The oceans had risen to create new waterfront properties on every continent, and William could see the breakers coming into shore from the Pacific about two blocks away. The bearded bro stared down at you from every street corner, and he was the only color in this frigid world of dark shadows. The hologram on the building across the street was looking right at him and broadcasting: BIG BRO IS MINDING YOU, the voice said, as the image's dark eyes looked deep into William's own. Down in the street, another poster, this one of paper, was whipping along in the wind, and William could see the letters YSW across the blue-green image of the world. In the far distance, a drone hovered and then darted, like a dragonfly, between the low hacienda-type tourist traps. They were protecting the inner party members, those aged 1-39, who took in the sights and sounds of old San Diego, completely protected by the drones, which could call in an air strike or a "droid doom boom" in seconds, to disperse an unruly mob or individual. The drone patrols didn't matter, however. Only the Mindfulness Droid Protectors, or MDP, mattered.

On another building made to resemble a Spanish restaurant, the same YSW news was being broadcast. The screen could transmit and receive simultaneously, and William knew all the spy devices could pick-up even a whisper from a citizen in the street. A young party member of about sixteen walked toward him, accompanied by two females. They were walking amidst the hundreds of tourists who were taking their children on a walking tour of the pseudo-Mexican structures that looked more like Big Bro's idea of what Hispanic culture was than what it actually had been. The three party members had their telescreen visors over their eyes, and yet the two women were topless and giggling, as the young stud between them masturbated in public to the pornography going on in his private 3D world of illusion. William shook his head in dismay as he passed them.

The world was now broken into pods of control called "Mindful Metro Campuses," and William was serving in the southern quadrant of what used be known as North America. The cities kept their names, and there were vague attempts at cultural identification, as it was in Old Town, but there was no longer any central government other than Big Bro and the Young Socialists World Party. After the War on Terror was declared victorious by the bands of millions of unemployed youth across the globe, in what was believed to be 2028, a new vision for the future was declared, and there was a unique coming together of computer and android technology and the vision of a powerful youth, who decided to snatch the wealth of their more primitive elders and construct a new world order. Religions were banned for the good of the libertarian principles espoused by the new party, and so were any sports, recreation, business or other human endeavor that seemed to promote any kind of collective values or principles other than what Big Bro was declaring as "the only path out of the chaos and militant fear that was our past."

Up ahead stood the tall skyscraper—the only one allowed—of the Young Socialists' Ministry of Mindfulness. This was where William worked, and it was also broadcasting the libertarian message of the party, in ten-foot letters, running every ten seconds across the huge digital banner in front of the building:

WAR IS IN THE PAST
FREEDOM IS ALWAYS TODAY
IGNORANCE IS IN WRITTEN HISTORY

The Ministry of Mindfulness contained four thousand rooms above ground and corresponding fortresses below. Scattered about San Diego, as in every other major metropolitan city in the world, were just three other buildings of the same appearance and size. They were the giants in the land of Lilliputian structures and hostels, and they were the only buildings allowed to be constructed above one story tall. These were the skyscrapers that housed the complete apparatus of government for Big Bro's Young Socialist World Party. The Ministry of Mindfulness, which controlled news, entertainment, meditation, education and the fine arts. The Ministry of Visual Reality, which ran the armies of drones and androids. The Ministry of Freedom, which concerned itself with suppressing any rebellions. And the Ministry of Living Bliss, which maintained economic affairs. Their names in Mindfulvoice: Minimind, Miniview, Minifree and Minibliss.

William knew that the Ministry of Freedom was the most frightening and sinister building. It had no windows, and it was kept in complete darkness inside, as everyone who entered was issued infrared gear and goggles to see. It was guarded 24/7 by android guards armed with laser bio-demobilizing rifles that could cause a human head to explode. You could enter and exit only after having been injected with top-secret computer chips from Big Bro's office inside.

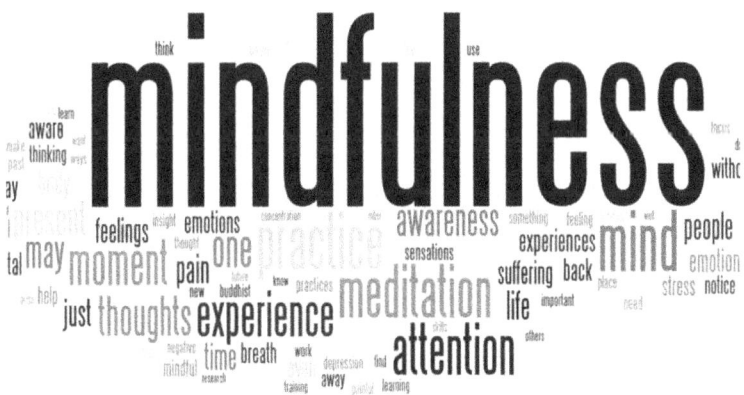

As he came near the Ministry of Mindfulness, William stopped to go into a small store maintained by one of the few middle-aged shopkeepers allowed to sell anything to younger party members. He had one android helper inside who came up to William when he stepped inside. By coming to work so late, William knew he had missed his chance at a free lunch in the Minimind canteen, but the food there was like eating laundry starch. "May I assist you?" the droid said. "Give me some Mindful Weed," William told him, "and one of those Big Bro Dogs," he added, pointing to some revolving wieners inside the microwave hotdog creator. The soy dog was placed on the bun, and given the usual relish, onion and mustard. William bent over the public hookah and took two hits off the marijuana. It was strong, and he coughed, but he felt almost instantly hungry. "Can I use your meditation room?" William asked the proprietor, a short man with an apron and receding hairline. His eyebrows were curling up on the ends, reminding William of his mother's stories of Mark Twain, the author. "Go ahead, young man," the man said. "I have to start the Minifree timer, however, as you must be out in an hour."

Inside the small back room, William turned on the LED lamp in the middle of the table as he munched on his Bro dog and turned on the spy camera deactivator that was issued only to party members who were aged 21-39. It was one of the perks of working for the Ministry of Mindfulness, and William used it for this purpose only. He then took out a black book from his inside coat pocket and opened it. His mother had taught him the craft of written language, which was strictly forbidden by the Ministry of Freedom, and he wrote the letters carefully, in block printing, as script writing had been prevented even in his mother's time: April 4th, 2050.

William leaned back in the metal chair. He felt completely powerless and doomed. For one thing, he didn't even know if this was actually 2050. It should be around that time, as his mother said he was 39, and he was born in the year 2013 or 2014. However, since the party had long ago destroyed calendars and any means of recording history, it was never possible these days to figure out what day it was within a year or two. Only the elders, like Rose, when she had her memory, and his father, John, could remember the past, and they were strictly confined to the Geriatric Units run by androids from the Ministry of Mindful Bliss and controlled by the Ministry of Freedom. William also knew that in three days he would be given the surname of his father: Drury. This was the moment chosen by the government to give all citizens a familial identity, as before that date, one was a completely free spirit who was supposedly not owned by any government entity or family unit. His father and mother told William that the slave owners had also given their slaves first names only, or they were forced to keep the owner's last name, but the slaves gave themselves unique names that only they used. Names such as: Sabe, Anque, Bumbo, Jobah, Quamana, Taynay, and Yearie. These names were used only inside the slave quarters, but it gave them some dignity to have chosen names rather than the assigned names of their owners.

Who the hell will read this diary, anyway? William thought. The future, according to Big Bro, was now. The visual was the only way one could communicate, as books on paper were forbidden, and his words would only be of interest to those who could remember the past. After he reached 40, he knew, the past would become only the bliss of the Eternal Now.

He sat gazing stupidly at his new journal for several minutes, eating up precious time. He knew he wanted to write about his mother and her dementia and about his father and what had happened before. The story he had told himself had been a constant monologue in his mind for years, but now he was dried up. His knee was pulsing with pain under the table, and he didn't want to be late for work. His mind was also a bit fractured from the hits of weed. He finally pulled out the sheet of paper that his father had written down for him to copy. William had smuggled it out of the Gerontology building four years earlier.

In an instant, he began writing, in panic, only half-aware of what he was putting down for history. His printing went all over the page and came in gasping scrawls. However, he wanted it there, and he wanted there to be some kind of historical record for all to see:

April 4, 2050. My father, John, gave me this story today from his confines in Minibliss Gerontology Unit 62. I want to write it down because these are his words, and he comes from a world of the past that revered stories and the words which recorded the paradoxical nature of the real world before Big Bro even existed. Here goes nothing:

After she read the story I had published in the college literary magazine, she announced to her sorority sisters that she was going to "marry that writer." Rose took my hand as we stood under the stars after the football game. This was before everything became black and white, so I could still see the yellowish tint of the full moon. Her hair was straightened and black, however, falling through my fingers like the strands of corn silk on my father's farm in Illinois. The colors were vivid that fall, red-orange leaf flames that whipped through the devil winds as we walked together. Day or night, our hands clasped together, back when it meant something to your heart's content to be together. We were dumbfounded during those hours on campus, walking to the rhythm of the cicadas, until her brown eyes began darting back and forth, and her Baptist upbringing brought her back to the world.

"I must get back to study," she would smile up at me at those moments, pursing her lips in preparation for the ritual kiss that our lips knew was coming. As my head moved down to meet those parted pillows of satiny moistness, a thought struck me, and I closed my eyes. Are my lips trained enough to find their way home to her? Is my love stronger than the pitch-black blindness of self-will run riot? I, too, wanted to run back to study my senses in front of a computer screen. The keys stretched under my poised hands like endless rows of QWERTY muscle memories. To reach my bliss, I had to always remember those lips of hers, and then I would plunge down into my subconscious to enter the raging flow of eternal sensation where colors meant nothing, and her body was mine in the dark.

Now. Today, I only leave her to walk outside onto the campus. We worked many years teaching their children how to form competent sentences on the pages of computer screens. As keepers of metaphor and simile, we were their momentary baptism into the world of the senses. Our three unit course called "Poetry and Literature Made Relevant for the Return to Nature" was required for graduation. It was the only chance our students got to study Jackson and her sensuous lottery, Richard Wright and Flannery O'Connor and their psychology of inner phantasms, or Edgar Allan Poe and Herman Melville and their dark shadows of murderous insanity. But they were not inside books that can be held in the hands. They were inside the scrolling digital distraction that has become the god to us all. There were no more contemporary authors who wrote for the inner world of the senses. No. Never again would these words do their job of reaching deep into the reader's sensual consciousness to manipulate the telltale heart, or to bathe in the mist of the rising great white whale, or to feel the strike of the first stone on the forehead of the chosen one. This was our job, and it was a brief one. When our students left our classes, they were once more enveloped in the "Mindfulness of the Real Moment," where literal memory was used as one uses a doorknob to enter another neat office, never again to see it open into a haunted house on a hill or into a damp dungeon whereupon a man was awaiting the slow, slicing downward doom of the pendulum blade, to open his chest and expose the throbbing crimson passion of his own heart. Hearts were to be measured, monitored and strengthened by exercise. Hearts had lost their metaphorical power over minds in the year 2028. The seat of power had made a seismic shift over the years until it was now the digital brain that held sway over all, *and all bowed down to its dominant scientific genius.*

The edict came down after we had retired from twenty-two years of teaching. Rose had fallen that same day in the middle of the lawn between her classes. It was to be the first fall of many, as she had contracted what we later discovered was Lewy Body Dementia. The edict came out, and I received the following explanation on my phone after Rose was diagnosed by Neurology. These rather dispassionate words were meant to assist me in my adventure living with her from that day forward:

SYMPTOMS EXPLAINED

In this section we'll discuss each of the symptoms, starting with the key word: dementia. Dementia is a process whereby the person becomes progressively confused. The earliest signs are usually memory problems, changes in their way of speaking, such as forgetting words, and personality problems. Cognitive symptoms of dementia include poor problem solving, difficulty with learning new skills and impaired decision making.

Other causes of dementia should be ruled out first, such as alcoholism, overuse of medication, thyroid or metabolic problems. Strokes can also cause dementia. If these reasons are ruled out then the person is said to have a degenerative dementia. Lewy Body Dementia is second only to Alzheimer's disease as the most common form of dementia.

Fluctuations in cognition will be noticeable to those who are close to the person with LBD, such as their partner. At times the person will be alert and then suddenly have acute episodes of confusion. These may last hours or days. Because of these fluctuations, it is not uncommon for it to be thought that the person is "faking". This fluctuation is not related to the well-known "sundowning" of Alzheimer's. In other words, there is no specific time of day when confusion can be seen to occur.

Hallucinations are usually, but not always, visual and often are more pronounced when the person is most confused. They are not necessarily frightening to the person. Other modalities of hallucinations include sound, taste, smell, and touch.

Parkinsonism or Parkinson's Disease symptoms, take the form of changes in gait; the person may shuffle or walk stiffly. There may also be frequent falls. Body stiffness in the arms or legs, or tremors may also occur. Parkinson's mask (blank stare, emotionless look on face), stooped posture, drooling and runny nose may be present.

REM Sleep Behavior Disorder (RBD) is often noted in persons with Lewy Body Dementia. During periods of REM sleep, the person will move, gesture and/or speak. There may be more pronounced confusion between the dream and waking reality when the person awakens. RBD may actually be the earliest symptom of LBD in some patients, and is now considered a significant risk factor for developing LBD. (One recent study found that nearly two-thirds of patients diagnosed with RBD developed degenerative brain diseases, including Lewy Body Dementia, Parkinson's disease, and multiple system atrophy, after an average of 11 years of receiving an RBD diagnosis. All three diseases are called synucleinopathies, due to the presence of a mis-folded protein in the brain called alpha-synuclein.)

SYMPTOMS EXPLAINED AFTER THE EDICT

Every person over the age of 65 now sees things in black and white. It is "understood" by the ruling youth party, the Young Democratic Socialists, that this is the most humane way to allow the elderly to adjust to the coming darkness of dementia, forgetfulness and decreasing energy caused by the depletion of dopamine and the crucial brain chemical acetylcholine.

My granddaughter, Esther, explained it to me one day while watching an old movie on her tablet. "Grandpa, you see old movies now, don't you? Is this why old people see only in black and white?"

Of course, I couldn't tell my granddaughter the truth. We elderly were being kicked to the side of life's road because we were getting in the way. Society had become a limitless range of physical experiences that required all one's senses in the REAL MOMENT. The state religion said so. There were no old religions that I could remember like Judaism, Islam, Buddhism or even my wife's Christianity. The only allowed religion, after the world's war on terror, was the secular religion of "Mindfulness."

When Mindfulness first became popular, my wife was already beginning to be a pariah to the new youth society. She could no longer work her computer or teach her students. She had fallen that morning in the bathroom and broken her hip, and there was to be no more walking for Rose. I tried to explain the image of the Mindful to her, but her mind was too confused to process it. The fluffy mats extended for acres across the field of green grass, as the edict had not come into effect, and we were only 61. The figures of healthy young bodies in yoga tops and pants were in the meditative positions of the present. Some were in full lotus, others were simply on their backs, staring up into the clouds overhead. But, it was definitely visible to me that their diaphragms were moving, in and out, like bellows. Over the loudspeaker, came the voice of the guru: BREATHE IN THE UNIVERSE, BREATHE OUT THE UNIVERSE. CONCENTRATE ON YOUR BREATH. KEEP CENTERED ON THE NOW, AS THERE IS NO OTHER REALITY ANYWHERE. NO TRANSIENT THOUGHTS. BANISH THEM LIKE THE FOUL, WRETCHED INTERLOPERS THEY ARE! YOU ARE CLEAN, PURE AND HEALTHY MESSENGERS OF FREEDOM. YOUR PRESENCE IS REAL, AND YOUR HEALTHY LIFE IS PRESENT IN ALL WE TOUCH, TASTE, SMELL AND VIEW. GOODNESS SURROUNDS YOU, AND GOODNESSS IS WITHIN YOU. FOREVER IS NOW!

I stumbled over to the bed and looked down at my wife. Her eyes were wide, and she mumbled, "Help me, John. I might fall off." Rose was in the exact center of the bed, *but her mind told her she was on the edge. Who does one trust? When does one stop trusting one's own mind? I am constantly telling her she has a disease that makes her mind tell her things that aren't real, but I also know that's my job. I attempt to convince readers that my fictions are real. I realize she needs my mindfulness right now more than any mindfulness that's outside our home in that youth culture all around us.*

I survive only as long as I can write the non-fiction stories they love, and teach them about how wonderful they are. They understand I am over the edge, at 65, and yet I am a bit of a darling to the Young Socialists. I suppose I'm rather like the pet Jews that were kept by the commandants of concentration camps in order to show to themselves they weren't really monsters after all. But I am an atheist, and I believe only in the senses. I perform my daily routine while the personal care android assists my wife in her routine. This is the only reality I know. There are no future convergences with the Cosmic Whole. There are no heaven or hell or even a purgatory, and there are certainly no religious beliefs worth dying for. The culture of youth stopped all of that. All is now programmed to affect the peaceful presence of the Eternal Now.

It is now night, and I am going to attend to the only duty that makes me an anathema to the world's youth. I am going to write my Report to the Artists. This is the only network communication that is allowed to be written in the "manner of the sensual lies," which was the method of artistic expression before our world changed into what it is today. My son, William, heir to my name, today works for the Ministry of Mindfulness, and this fact allows me the freedom to create my stories to other artists.

Rose is sleeping, and her wondrous lips bid me farewell as she mumbles her RBD dreams. I kiss them, and I can see a smile form, like the rising of the full moon, and I am again yearning for the only sanity I have left.

As I walk toward my little room down the hall of our campus unit, I wait for my gait to become impeded. If I fall, if I hit my head, if my hip is shattered, I will be rushed like all of the rest to the local Emergency Room. Although medical care is now free to all, it has become biased toward youth. There are, of course, the duplicants, the androids, the ones who keep the world at peace each day. Without them, the culture of youth would not be allowed to flourish and prosper. The expense of repairing the elderly has become a burden to the world's economy. We are no longer part of the medical android programming, except for patching us up and sending us on our way. Wisdom is no longer the province of the old. Instead, all that is good and sensuous is to be lived in the present moment and not in the heads of some old storytellers like me. Analysis and android workers are meant to keep the young strong and to keep the old moving forward to their inevitable doom.

I am one of the tokens left over from the past. I am the keeper of "fiction." There is no word like that anymore. Once, when I was young, the world allowed the stories to *be told at deeper levels than on the screen. In our books, we could experience the moment-by-moment sensual present as a masterful invention by authors. Today, my Blog of Sensual Lies is visited by those who are old, like me, and we share in my memories and in my fears. We are allowed to do this because the culture of youth no longer fears our power over the senses. Books long ago became relics from the Age of Fear, when history was manipulated by writers, and entertainment could be found in the intimate dance between writer and his reader. I can't remember the day fiction books were banned because when I turned 65, I was given the implant that all the elderly must receive.*

As I entered the darkened room, my study, I could see the screen once more. It was bold and white, opened to the word processing software from the bygone years when my stories meant something to me and to my readers. Today, my words were simply anachronistic writhing on the page sent out from my academic unit to soothe the tired minds of a dying breed: the artists. I have only 623 subscribers to my blog. I have never met a single one. They visit my virtual world only because they can, like me, remember those days when writers, visual artists and even poets, produced singular works that were theirs alone, and these sensually provocative creations were shared, or published, to others inside book stores, libraries, art galleries and over the Internet. The youth culture and the Mindful World of the Eternal Now have banished us to this tiny island of reality. My screen beckoned me, and I sat down again to create and to listen.

November 20, 2028, San Diego.

I sat inside the student center today and listened. The clicking of keyboards, the words of half-conversations, the chanting and breathing of those in meditation. There was no story there because my senses were in the real moment, the moment in my mind. This was like the moments I dreaded on the farm, back when farms were still places to manage and to provide for a family.

Rose stands beside the gate, posing for a picture. I brought her home from college to meet my parents. My father holds the digital camera in his big hands, and my mother is whispering to him. Rose was a city girl and a Baptist, and my mother's mouth moved in rapid undulations, and I knew she didn't like my new wife. I moved over to stand beside them as we watched Rose standing in front of the milk cows, looking behind her every five seconds to see what the cows were doing. Rose was not the picture of a farm girl. Mother's smile broke out like a nervous reaction to the poisonous words she was whispering. 'She's a princess. A libertine. She'll never make a good mother with her liberal attitudes and her literary snobbery.'

When the war on terror ended, in 2028, my mother, Janice, embraced the new youth party with enthusiasm. She sat around all day in the shade of our big oak tree, riding the creaking swing on the big branch, as the new androids rushed around doing all the chores on her farm. A week after the androids took over, my father, Gerald, was found inside the barn swinging below the entrance to the hayloft. Rudy, our farm hand, told me later that he found a book next to the milking stool my father used to push off from. It was a novel by Thomas Hardy called Far from the Madding Crowd. My father had always identified with the character of Gabriel, the shepherd. The cows were his sheep. "When Mr. Gerry saw that android herd his cows into the milking stalls, his face looked like the time you fell out of the oak tree and broke your leg. After the android hooked them up to the new high-speed WiFi milking machines, Mr. Gerry walked down the rows of cows and unhooked each of the titanium vacuums from the teats. He kept yelling, 'Free at last, free at last, thank God almighty, free at last!' After the big android started up again the next day, with new programming to prevent Mr. Gerry from getting in the way, Mr. Gerry had declared all-out war. He had a big scythe from the loft in his hands, and when the android turned on the WiFi to send the titanium vacuums out like snakes to find the teats of those cows, your papa began swinging. But the android was fast, and it was strong. It blasted a big net that shot out from its metallic body and covered Mr. Gerry's full human body. He looked like a fly in a spider web. When the milking was done, Mr. Gerry was still sobbing under that net on the floor of the barn. After the android left, I took the net off of him, and he stood up. He picked out all the hay from his hair and beard, and he stood straight as a lightning rod. 'The new sheepdog has run my cattle over the cliff and into the sea,' he said, and the next morning, I found him hanging in the barn when I was bringing in the cattle to be milked."

PICKING QUARRELS AND PROVOKING TROUBLE! THIS WEBSITE IN VIOLATION OF YDS CODE 4628-25.

When I saw these words flash onto my screen, I stood up and tried to run to the door. Down the hall I heard the door open. The telltale whir and whoosh. The two android guards burst into my den and grabbed onto my arms. They were black and white, of course, but my memory gave me an inside picture of Darth Vader's black, wheezing form instead of the moment-to-moment reality of the lithe, titanium bodies of the two guards. I could hear their humming processors, and I could feel the pressure of the hand of one of them as it came up behind my head. The puncture was like the diabetic injection I gave Rose twice daily. When the drug entered my system, I became attuned to the present, and my artist's emotional reality became lost in the Eternal Now.

THE CLASSROOM LESSON

The Guru of the Present Moment turned to the class. He was waving a scanner over the prone body of Professor John Drury, who had the blank stare of dementia so often seen in victims of old age. Old Professor Drury had recently taught the antiquated class "Poetry and Literature Made Relevant for the Return to Nature," which had now been exorcised from the curricula.

The new teacher was an android of the latest design, and it almost looked human, with its pink flesh, arching eyebrows and smoothly dignified gestures. But, if one looked carefully, the eyes gave its reality away. The pupils were blinking, off and on, with a pulsating rhythm of an inner perfection not known to humankind.

The voice of the guru sounded authentically human, and his slight British inflection made the students pay attention because it was just like the voice of the new reality show host, Prince Hal, who could speak in every language of the globe and could dance every dance popular over the Youth Wide World Jam Time Music Network.

"Learn to turn to each person as the most sacred person on Earth, to each moment as the most sacred moment that has ever been given to us. Then perhaps we are awake a bit more, perhaps breathing together with God."

This was the oath of every health worker in the YDS from the new Ministry of Mindful Bliss. It was recited every time a new elder was being transitioned into the care of the android nurses in the Gerontology units.

These androids were managed by the students in this class, and Professor Drury was there as a demonstration of what humane care for the elderly should be like within these compounds. As the voice of the guru droned on in objective and analytical preciseness, the mind of the good professor was taking off on its own.

Up into the black and white room, his mind rose, over the

heads of these human computers, through the walls that could not contain his spirit. The spirit of the mind of an artist was not bound by any science, formula or algorithm.

Above the campus, he looked down. The rows of buildings, perfectly lined and ordered, the fields of athletic youth playing for the joy of competition and not for the harsh preparations for war. It was very beautiful to him, and he smiled down on them. The chaos of his life had disappeared with the transitional surgery, and he was now ready for the final release.

But, breaking through this paradise came those same lips. She was down there, in one of the buildings, calling out his name, 'John! I'm falling! Please! Help me!'

Down he sped, toward the glowing white-hot light inside the building at the end of the row. Rose's lips parted, and she was speaking to him. The voice came from a spirit world that was perhaps destroyed on their level, but this new level of the unconscious was slowly taking form inside her brain.

When their lips met, their daughter, Ruth, was giving birth to their granddaughter, Esther. Then Esther was walking, parading before the adults with her tablet, working on a secret code to be used as she grew to be a young child and then an adult. The code was formulated perfectly, and it was a virus that would soon be inside every digital network in the world, releasing the masses from the prisons of perfection they had created, and leaving on their screens a message that had bound her grandparents, John and Rose, together inside the world of sensual imagination:

'There is an almost sensual longing for communion with others who have a larger vision. The immense fulfillment of the friendships between those engaged in furthering the evolution of consciousness has a quality almost impossible to describe.'

Their lips met, the virus became live, and the colors rushed in. All the world's youth, one by one, broke free from their self-imposed chains to live once more, openly, in chaotic joy and sensuous wonder. They ran to the elderly and the infirm to release them and to listen quietly for the stories to begin once more, in the darkness of evening, before sleep overtook them again.

The Guru of the Present Moment spoke again to his students, "Hallucinations are usually, but not always, visual and often are more pronounced when the person is most confused. They are not necessarily frightening to the person. Other modalities of hallucinations include sound, taste, smell, and touch. We try to make them as physically comfortable as possible while they are going through this mental agony."

William stopped writing because his hand was cramping, but his story was completed. He tore his father's writing into small pieces and shoved them inside his mouth. As he chewed, he could feel the time ticking down, and he knew he must get to work. He swallowed, with some effort, and tucked his black diary back inside his coat pocket. The buzzer ending his hour sounded, and he left the room.

William arrived on the fifteenth floor of the Ministry of Mindfulness at eleven hundred. He worked in the Department of Visual Reality Recordings, and all of his colleagues were dragging metal chairs outside in the hall to face the wide digital screen on the wall at the end of it. They were preparing for the Mindfulness Meditation. William took his place in one of the center rows. As he adjusted the back of his injured knee on the metal seat, he saw two people he knew by sight but had never met personally. One was a young, fierce-looking girl in her late twenties, who worked in the Erotica and Romance Department. He believed she was a computer technician, as he had seen her with USB drives on several occasions. He knew that these trashy video stories were created by computer, as all the plots were the same, and the programmed details were inserted into the visuals as one would assemble a Big Bro hotdog. The youth gobbled these stories up like hotdogs, however, and they kept them entertained because they were also infused with accompanying music and audio soundtracks. She wore the red skirt of the Youthful Sensual Bliss Alliance, so she was most likely one of the staunch adherents to the Party of Big Bro. Her black hair was naturally frizzy, and the freckles on her chocolate cocoa butter face made her look like a country girl from William's birth state of Illinois. However, she had once given him such a cold and piercingly dreadful stare in the hallway that he had thought she might be one of the latest Mindfulness Droid Protectors sent to spy on them by the Ministry of Freedom.

The other person was a man called Thornton, a member of the Founding Youth Party, who held a post that was so important that William had only a vague idea of what it might be. He looked about twenty-five, and his face held the quiet confidence of one of the ones who had first formulated the philosophical underpinnings that ruled daily life all over the world. He had the muscular physique of one who did daily workouts in the Big Bro

Workout Studio, filled with all kinds of computerized exercise equipment. His face had the blond, look-alike beard of Big Bro that many men in the inner party fashioned for themselves. Thornton also had the habit of whistling the latest popular tunes so well that others would stop in the hall to listen to him. In fact, over the years that William had seen him at work, Thornton seemed somehow more accessible than most inner party members. Perhaps it was his smile and casual manner. Maybe it was the way he intelligently laughed at the stupid ads that come over the news channel. At any rate, Thornton decided to wait with the brothers and sisters in William's department until the Mindfulness Meditation was completed because he sat in the chair next to William and smiled over at him. The Erotica and Romance girl was sitting right behind them in the same row.

William expected the same ritual procedure in the meditation. It did begin in the usual way, with the figure of Big Bro coming out to sit on his gold yoga mat, center stage. The background was a pale, robin's egg blue, and their leader seemed his usual tranquil self as he crossed his legs in the full lotus and smiled out at them. The sitar music in the background was playing, and when he spoke, blond beard's voice had its usual flair for the dramatic. William always thought it sounded more like a voice to sell breakfast cereal than a voice to calm the human mind.

"Brothers and sisters, I want you to breathe deeply and focus upon the infinite moment of the present. Are we not fortunate to have world peace at last, under the guidance of our party, as children are being born into a free society, which gives them opportunities that have never existed before? But before I begin our guided transcendence, I want to warn you all of an underground movement that the Ministry of Freedom has discovered exists in your campus pod of San Diego!

The screen went dark for a moment, and then the face of William's father, John, appeared, in a full-face close-up. William choked once and began to cough so long and violently that Thornton reached over and patted him on the back several times.

Big Bro spoke over John Drury's image. "This man, John Alfred Drury, has been used by certain individuals as the focus of rebellion. It seems he wrote a certain printed text called *The Insane Call Us Free,* which has been circulating throughout our campus for over a week. We want to confiscate any copies that may be in your possession, so there will be a full court press to discover those brothers and sisters who have read this book and who might be aware of its circulation and the copies that are out there. As you know, ever since we came to power to suppress those elderly warmongers who always sent the young out to die for their politically and industrially complex causes, there have been groups that arose to rebel against us. They want to return us to the days when wartime fever gave meaning to them and gave them the anger and fear they needed to send our young into battle! Thanks to our victory in 2028, we no longer have a wartime society. However, this cancerous book must be found and destroyed! Its author was once a collegiate educator who taught our young, and now his secret book is being used to attack us and perhaps raise enough support to mount some kind of counter-revolution. Can we allow this?"

"No! To hell with Dr. Drury and his book!" our unit of brothers and sisters shouted back at the screen.

"We never want to return to this!" said Big Bro, and the screen then filled with videos from the past before 2028. Drone strikes sent Peacekeeper missiles into the homes of villages. Villagers screamed over the bloody bodies lined up by the hundreds and raised their fists to the sky. Kneeing citizens in orange smocks were beheaded out in the town squares, places of religious worship, over television, and inside soccer stadiums. Millions of refugees fled the wars all over the world, dying in rat-infested boats and perishing inside other dangerous vehicles of transport. The insane killings of lone wolf terrorists also filled the screen with horror.

Then, just as quickly, the sounds of waterfalls and sitar music returned, and the calm smile of Big Bro broke wide across the screen. "How can this one man accuse us of being the insane killers? We, who bring peace and brotherhood to the Planet Earth! Let us meditate on the face of this Dr. Drury. Focus on his features and memorize this book and its title. If any brother should mention his name or discuss the contents of this book to you, you must report him or her to the nearest Minifree official.

The rest of the meditation was the constipated sound of "auuuummmm" coming from Big Bro and the haggard face of William's father, Dr. John Drury, staring back at all of them, like some kind of crazy black heretic. As the face returned to Big Bro, the Party slogans once more appeared in bold capitals:

WAR IS IN THE PAST
FREEDOM IS ALWAYS TODAY
IGNORANCE IS IN WRITTEN HISTORY

William stood up at his seat as the lights came back on in the hallway. In three days' time, he would become William Drury, as his very own Department of Visual Reality Recordings would present the video of his birth, along with the names of his mother and father, to be officially entered into the Ministry of Freedom's records for the rest of his natural life. And, at that same moment, he would also become one of the most dangerous members of society. As his mind filled with hatred for Big Bro, the Party, and for those secret spies around him, William also began to visualize a new hatred, and he turned around to stare directly into the brown eyes of the frizzy-headed black girl from the Department of Erotica and Romance. He wanted to grab her by the hair and drag her screaming out into the night, out into the tourist traps of Old Town, forcing her to fellate him in public, as he shouted obscenities about how blacks were still being subjected to forced labor and demeaning jobs. He heard his voice inside his mind as he stared hard at those young brown eyes of the enemy: *See this young and healthy black woman? She creates the visual pornography that greases the coffers of the Ministry of Living Bliss. Her face is black, and my face is black. Together, with our parents behind us, we serve as the scapegoats to your Big Bro and his lying peaceful coexistence. You thought we brought rape and gang violence to your cities? Well, now you're going to see what we can do for this peaceful land of the guru pods and frat boy parties! Here comes the rebel forces, and the black history of true freedom shall lead us!*

The black woman from Erotica and Romance left the room. However, as he turned back around, he caught the eye of Thornton standing next to him. The big man had been watching him as William had been going through his hate passion. Of course, it had only been in his mind, but still, there must have been some anger showing on his face as he thought his traitorous thoughts and indicted the Party and Big Bro with his venomous accusations. Thornton was smiling at him with recognition, as if to say, "I'm with you!" It was only a transient moment's glance, and then Thornton turned away from William and began his slow trek back to the upper offices of the inner party.

Later, back inside his hostel room, William was thinking about the day's events while holding his pen in his right hand. He was using the rest of his privacy spy camera deactivation chips. Party members who worked at the Ministry of Mindfulness were given six chips for the year as a way to claim that they were special people to the inner Party. William's eyes returned to the page in his diary, and he discovered he had been doing some automatic printing in all caps:

FUCK BIG BRO
FUCK BIG BRO
FUCK BIG BRO
FUCK BIG BRO
FUCK BIG BRO

These words covered almost an entire page, and his mind immediately filled him with fear. It was crazy, as those words were not any more dangerous than when he had first taken the pages from his father inside the gerontology unit. Just for a few seconds, William thought he should tear-up the diary and try to escape San Diego forever before his name became recorded. He realized that this kind of escape was even more insane than his father's book being written.

Everyone knew how these things went down. Whether he wrote down FUCK BIG BRO, or whether he did not, it made no difference. Whether he continued writing inside his diary or mounted a revolt against the Party, it made no difference. The secret police unit of Mindfulness Droid Protectors, the MDP, would arrest him. He had committed a crime just by being born. His father had told him about the days in the past, when there were the wars, that his people had been condemned by society even if they served to fight the enemy, or did not serve to fight the enemy. More black young men were arrested than any other races, and white citizens ran to other sides of the streets when you were walking down them, and they shot you before you could surrender, and they kept you down until you gave up trying to improve your life. Father had been secluded inside the halls of academia, and yet he still understood the wall of fear and resentment built up around his black community. That same fear had finally returned to the "eternally peaceful now," as Big Bro phrased it, and Drury was chosen to be the scapegoat for an entire generation of leaders. William now wondered how many in the inner founding party were black. Thornton was certainly not. Perhaps he could find out before it was over and they shot him in the back of the head, just like they did to all the other traitors.

The arrests always come at night—just the way his father told him the white Klansmen had come during the olden days. You were jerked from a sound sleep, the calloused hand grabbed your shirt and yanked you to your feet. They shook you, and their LEDs lit your eyes, the ring of frowning faces circling your bed like vultures around their carrion. His father told him that there was once a law called a "patriot act," and people of color had also been rounded up to be kept in prison with no trial, just the way the Party did things today. Men were often singled out as world terrorists and shot from drones that hovered above them in the clear skies of many foreign lands. Again, no trials, no arguments, no fuss, and no muss. It seemed, said John Drury that the Party had learned its lessons well from the past and had actually not forgotten these methods of maintaining "freedom" around the world. In today's system of peacekeeping justice, there was also never any trial for the accused. If you were labeled a terrorist to the State, you instantly became a hunted creature, just like a rogue elephant terrorizing a peaceful village, or a man-eating lion sneaking into a hut by the full moon. In fact, today, there was no report of the arrest. Since you spent most of your life with no surname, it was that much easier to erase you from all records. Your name was removed, every record disappeared, always during the night. For, in the morning, there appeared the great sun of new beginnings in the Eternal Now, beaming out at his family and guiding them in the peaceful morning's meditations. The State religion was Mindfulness, and William worked for it, and he was now going to be arrested, without a trial, and then become vaporized, abolished or annihilated, although "vaporized" was the most popular term used. William imagined it was because of how efficient the system worked to move its citizens toward death and complete disappearance forever—like the misty vapor of the marine layer over San Diego disappearing with the sun.

William was most afraid of the fact that he knew of no book written by his father entitled *The Insane Call Us Free.* The only books he knew written by his parents were articles on the great works of literature and the methodology of teaching the youth in the Party. His parents never discussed politics at home, and the only way William had discovered what his father knew about the past was when he turned 65 and was put into the gerontology units. Something had snapped inside, and John Drury began writing down his thoughts and memories on sheets of paper that William had smuggled into him from Minimind. Paper was used on a very limited basis. Only Big Bro approved posters and edicts were written on paper, and William was able to steal some of those sheets for his father to use. Today, with his 40th birthday just three days away, William had decided that he would also begin to write down his observations in a diary.

Perhaps the Party spies had found something William was not aware existed. If his father had indeed written such a book that slandered the Party and its practices, then there must be somebody else assisting him. William's mind again saw the face of Thornton, and he imagined if there were some inner party official who would do such a thing, he would be the type. The idea itself made William shiver and look back at the news screen on his wall. On the other hand, it was probably more likely the Party had decided to make a scapegoat of his father because of the website he had published for artists. Artistic expression was controlled expressly by the Ministry of Mindfulness, William's employer, and he had warned his father on several occasions to stop the communications on his blog. His father believed his writings were no threat to the government, and he also believed his favorite status among the young college students would protect him from scrutiny. He was obviously wrong, and now William was to be the next rebel placed on the roster of insurrectionists, unless he could do something to prevent the inevitable arrest.

His door began to vibrate from the pounding fist on its surface. *Are they arresting me now?* William thought, shoving his opened diary under the mattress on his cot.

S tanding in the hall were two co-workers with whom William had worked on a few projects at Minimind. Timothy and Ronda were 25 and 22 years of age, and they still had the beaming glow of optimism that most brothers and sisters were filled with after their indoctrination in college. As William looked back on his education, and compared it with what his parents had told him about their experiences, college today was more of a social festival so as to learn the ways one can survive in the world of Big Bro rather than a place where one's mind was given free rein to explore the Liberal Arts, whatever those were.

Willie!" said Timothy, grabbing William's hand, "come with us to a party in your honor at Casa de Pico. We've got almost all of the department to go, and there'll be free weed and presents. You'll be 40 in three days. I'm sure you're aware of that fact."

William knew if anybody could get their fellow workers together for anything, it would be Timothy and Ronda. They saw themselves as self-appointed social butterflies of the Party, as they were completely liberated sexually, and this was a feature that was especially promising in politics. William saw they were true to form today, as Timothy wore elevator heels that could be changed remotely from flats to heels, and a sequined evening gown with LED lights imprinted in thousands of flashing red and blue neon beads across his waist, with the grinning image of Big Bro serving as a glowing sash. The right side of Timothy's black face was made-up with rouge, mascara and lipstick, and his left side was his usual masculine glow of youth. His Afro fit both sexes, so that was quite appropriate for his bi-sexual role. He was muscular and moved inside a room like a black panther, which, coincidentally, William's father told him used to be a radical Black Power group in the United States. Having never seen a political Black Panther, however, Timothy was more in tune with Rainer Maria

Rilke's poetic version of the panther in the Paris zoo and "his limber lope, his softly-powerful paces back and forth." Ronda was also going with the split-identity look, but her top half was outfitted in the orange-glow jumpsuit of the Mindfulness Droid Protectors and her bottom half was the red yoga pants of Big Bro, complete with a pattern of Young Socialists of the World globes scattered like polka dots all over the velvet material. Her mirror shiny MDP black jackboots completed the ensemble.

William grabbed his worn grey windbreaker with the Minimind decal before he followed his two friends out the door. Timothy was doing his usual chattering as they walked down Congress Street toward the restaurant on the corner of Old Town Avenue. The wind had died down, but the sharp cold filled William's nostrils as he breathed in the sewage-laced odor from the ocean nearby.

"Did you hear about Roger? He was caught by the MDP teaching his section of middle youth about how to hack into the game site. They injected him with a blocker for six months. You know how social Roger is. Ronda thinks it will kill him." Timothy whirled around to face her.

"William is well aware of the ways of the MDP. Roger lives and dies online. He never really got any older than the tweens he supposedly educates. Without his telecommunal visor and phone, his mind will shrink like a marshmallow in a vacuum chamber. Not that he had much in his brain besides what Minimind gave him," Ronda said, raising up her jackboots in front of her in a mock imitation of the MDP march.

"It's sad to see," William said, "those blocked outer Party members can't communicate with anybody, and when you see them outside they look like electronic ghosts. Do they see us the same way we see them?"

"Of course, Willie! But I'm a much handsomer ghost than most. Those MDP get instant messages from any member who sees a violation occurring, and of course there are those drones all over the fucking place." Timothy spread his arms out to imitate one of the Minifree drones. Just as he did this, as if on cue, a black drone whirred down at them from the misty overcast of the marine layer.

"I think they're much more fun on the Great Drone Escape Race. Did you see the team from Carlsbad last week? They used laser pens to blind the drones, and they made it past the manure dump." Ronda was putting her hands beside her ears and sticking out her tongue at the hovering drone. After a few seconds, the drone rose a few feet and then shot off to the right toward the tourist shops on Old Town Avenue.

"I'm sorry, but I detest those things," William said. "Also, I hope you don't have anything special planned at this roast. Because I know you two. Nothing happens without the scathing sarcasm you seem to secrete from your bodies like sweat after a Big Bro workout."

Timothy giggled and did a pirouette on the balls of his heels. "Oh, William, my lad. I have no idea what you mean!"

William was pleased, despite the running warnings going on inside his head about his father and Big Bro's edict. Inside the restaurant, Senor Esparza kept the authentic idea of Mexico as it used to be alive. There was even a mariachi band to greet them as they entered the reserved dining room in the back, and the vibrant brass instruments from an ancient land enveloped William's consciousness like a warm blanket. The musicians wore all black, with silver studs adorning the sides of their pants, and they sported the tall hats and long mustaches of Pancho Villa vintage.

Esparza came up to them grinning like the Cheshire Cat. "*Muchachos y muchachas!* We have everything tonight. Thanks to Mr. Thornton, we have no soy meat. We have real beef and poultry—yes! Tacos, enchiladas, chilles rellenos, handmade tortillas, guacamole and salsa, it's all here, my friends, for you to enjoy, *con mucho gusto!*"

Thornton? William had never heard of anybody from the Inner Party attending a celebration for an outer member. Perhaps he was right about Thornton being sympathetic toward him. Why else would he have done all this? William's eyes scanned the room like a spy camera. There were about twenty or so members of his work group there, quite a big turn-out. Maybe the word got out about Thornton and the real meat. However, as per usual, most of them were standing alone, hiding inside their media visors or on their phones conversing with somebody more important than their boring colleagues in the eternal now. As for Thornton, he had yet to make an appearance.

Timothy and Ronda stood in the center of the room and addressed the collection of media zombies. It was a futile effort, as most of the audience kept their attention on their collection of noisy programs and music from the wonderful world Ministry of Mindfulness and its "cornucopia of super-max entertainment made just for you." Of course, William knew, all of the crap that was spewed forth had little intellectual content other than to be programmed titillations that were created after careful monitoring of the throbbing sex organs and love affairs of brothers and sisters on the joined Network of Eternal Bliss. Or else, there were the mindless games of chance and races to defy the odds of Big Bro's technology. The Minimind liked these types of competitions because they served as a sly method to get new ways to enforce their tools of oppression. When those team members in the Great Drone Escape Race used their penlight lasers, some Droid was secretly creating a way to combat such rebellious inventions. Most of these digital monkeys were too stupid to realize what was happening and what part they were playing in the overall plan to steal their creativity.

The same was true in the arenas of education, business and local government. All human members had to sign strict non-disclosure agreements and contracts that made everything they invented or even thought about on the job property of Big Bro and its worldwide tentacles of influence. And the MDP was always there to enforce those agreements.

"It's time to pay tribute to the man of the hour, the one who will soon be walking down that last mile to enter into the bliss of the next stage in life. He's been a personal friend of mine for the last four years, and he helped me learn how to work the Wi-Fi wipe and flush in the Minimind washrooms! Of course, I had the cleanest testicles I ever thought a guy could have until I got the hang of it. What can you say about a guy who visits his parents every week but tried kicking a goal on a secret field that was covered with gopher holes? The result was gophers 3 and William nothing but a sprained knee. Before we have him up here to receive his gifts, I want to declare the weed bar open! With all this great food provided courtesy of Mr. Jack Thornton, we can be thankful for Big Bro and the world peace we have enjoyed for over twenty years, and all the prosperity given freely to the brothers and sisters who apply the same plan for success that has been our salvation! Mind Big Bro, Mind Big Bro!" Timothy started the chant, and most of the workgroup took it up as they got into the line at the hookah, next to the room entrance, to take their turns inhaling hits. "Mind Big Bro! Mind Big Bro! Mind Big Bro!"

At that moment of the eternal now, the room began to vibrate, and the music erupted into the romantic strains of Wagner's *Tristan und Isolde*. The Mindfulness Droid Protectors, two of them, slid over the air in front of Jack Thornton, their orange jumpsuits shimmering under the neon of the restaurant lighting, their muscular arms locked over their laser rifles like corpses inside a vertical coffin. These were not the life-like, humanoid droids that ran most of the daily business of Big Bro. No, these were the Special Forces droids who were built to appear menacing, and their faces had been constructed with horror and fear in mind. Actually, they had two faces, one on the back of the head and one on the front. Both were colorful clown faces, with a perpetual grin, although one could see the razor-sharp document grinders sparkling behind the thick red lips under the red-bulb noses. These grinders were used to devour any printed matter not approved by the Ministry of Mindfulness.

William knew the faces of the MDP were clownish because Big Bro believed the little children would not be as frightened, but the idiots in the Inner Party obviously forgot about the razor teeth. These kinds of mixed messages were the rule rather than the exception with the government, and William understood them well. He watched with interest as Thornton stepped up on the riser to speak to his audience. The MDP droids stood at attention on either side of him and smiled out at the group of workers. As he was pretty whacked from the Mindful weed, William half-expected the droids to start making balloon animals to entertain the digital monkeys who were ignoring the speaker's words. Jack Thornton's face was handsome and smiling as he gazed out at their group, and when he clicked on his speaker voice megaphone button implanted on the side of his throat, his voice was clear and loud. Only Inner Party members had these devices, and they used them for such occasions in order to be heard over the white noise and media chaos of the moment. Thornton also had to now contend with the stoned members of the department, and keeping their attention was not an easy task.

"Mindfulness is your job, and mindfulness is at the center of our entire world order. Without the basic philosophy of our society, we would soon erode back into the chaos of war and the nationalism of our forefathers. Thanks to you and your tireless efforts, we can transfer each member of society into the mindful and blissful state of elder brothers and sisters. William, who has honored you by working on projects as diverse as the *True Vision of Big Bro at Home,* and the popular *Music Mindfulness to Increase Worker Productivity,* will soon be making his existential journey into the honored halls of the Inner Party to be recorded and given his surname. This is the name that will stamp him with the approval of the millions who have gone before him and who have also distinguished themselves by serving Big Bro with devotion and creativity. Please, William, come up here and say a few words, won't you?"

William didn't expect this. His throat tightened, and his heart began pounding in his chest as he walked up to the riser and climbed the three steps. "You'll have to speak loudly, William," Thornton winked at him as William faced his fellows, who were busy devouring the mounds of tacos and enchiladas, and who were obviously not paying any attention to him. Only Timothy and Ronda were dancing in front of them, like two court jesters. Timothy had two taquitos stuffed up each nostril, and Ronda was marching in front of the MDP droids and trying to make them smile to expose their titanium grinders.

Maybe it was the weed, or perhaps it was the moment of the eternal now that had been working at his consciousness all these years, but William decided to begin a debate with Big Bro and all he represented, through this tall and handsome emissary, Jack Thornton. His mind collected the main points he wanted to put forth, and then his dry mouth opened. His voice, at first, was a squeaky tremor, but as he got into his diatribe, it became clearer and more confident.

"Workers of the world unite! You have nothing to lose but your chains! Do those statements sound familiar at all to you? They come from a book my father gave me to read when I was ten years old. Yes, I said book. It had a cover, and it had paper pages, and it was bound with glue, and the words didn't scroll down endlessly on the page. It had form, and it had order, and it was meant to be kept and studied by people who could pass it amongst themselves, quote from it, pointing down at the text, getting angry and going on a tirade, possibly even believing what it said enough to mount a revolution in the street! It was part of a manifesto written by two men in 1848, and they were named Karl Marx and Friederich Engels. My question to you, Mr. Thornton, is this. Why is Big Bro so afraid of printed books?" William took a deep breath and waited. He expected Thornton to immediately turn the MDP droids on him, but all the handsome man did was smile down at William, and the smile on his face was not condescending. It was, as a matter of fact, fatherly and wise.

"Thanks for that question, William. You have hit upon one of the most important cornerstones of our party's philosophy. Alas, we usually don't explain such ideas to the masses, but since I know you at the Ministry of Mindfulness work daily on the communications that go out to all, I want to give you the explanation of this rule so you will understand it. Printed matter is dangerous because it can be used by individuals to mount campaigns, create laws and send people to prisons. In the historical context of the not-too-distant past, society was a collection of these printed monstrosities that filled our libraries and businesses with an endless collection of useless rules and regulations. The young people were the first to see how much time and wasted energy were being spent minding these collections. We created the digital copies with care and precision. The Inner Party now keeps all these records on file to remind us of how purposely confusing life was in the past. Why was it purposeful confusion? Because the nation-states wanted to maintain control over you through armies and weapons of mass destruction, and they wanted to allow the citizens to collect private stores of weapons so as to provide an endless variety of killing sprees and bloodbaths in the shopping malls, schools, churches and places of government. We have a visual record of all that was taking place in those years, and it's not a pretty sight! In fact, the Department of Visual Reality first began as a repository of history, so we would always be reminded of how cruel and heartless the past was. It was then called a free and open society, but it was actually a locked-down culture of repressed sexual desires and religious fanaticism. They imprisoned more citizens for drug violations than for any other infraction. Big Bro represents a step into the light of true freedom. We no longer repress individual freedoms, but we do restrict the freedom to kill one's brother or sister. Why? Because we love you! We also restrict printed materials because they can be used as tokens of rebellion, just as they were used in your father's time, William. I am not disparaging your father's past, William, I am simply pointing out the fact that his eyes were perhaps seeing through a rose-colored, academic hue. Big Bro, in his infinite wisdom, saw that the only thing we can control with any reasonable authority is the present. This is the dictum that has kept us together, and it will be the dictum that keeps us at peace all over the world!"

The audience was beginning to tire; some were actually slumping over at their tables, but William was just beginning to argue, and his face contorted with the explosion of repressed thoughts building up for years under Big Bro's regime.

"Why are you constantly spying on us if we're free? Why is our job at Minimind to monitor the shopping habits, the breeding habits and the thinking habits of our citizens and then to create the online control mechanisms to keep them unaware of the real hidden agenda? I believe the hidden agenda of Big Bro is to collect the wealth made from our digital entertainment devices and pour it into the coffers of the Inner Party. I believe you, Jack Thornton, and others in the Inner Party, have the largesse of our hard work secretly stashed in private banks around the world, and you are all enjoying your wealth at the expense of our actual freedoms! Go ahead! Arrest me. I've been waiting for this moment all my life. I know what turning 40 means. There is no bliss to enter into. I've seen these respected elders of your society. They drag themselves through the streets, empty smiles of insane atrophy on their faces, and you call it bliss. If they're lucky, some can run your government stores to sell trinkets and dispense the government's THC, but it is all, in actuality, controlled by the armies of droids you have at your disposal. My father told me you once mounted an armed campaign against the humans whose jobs were being taken by these droids. Where did the bodies go of those who died resisting your take-over, Mr. Thornton? Can you digitally copy actual human bodies now? No, I suppose that's next on your agenda. If Big Bro can block us off the grid of your free network, then I suppose he can eventually make us all into digital copies. Our recorded brains can perhaps become little tokens of memories to be enjoyed by candlelight, as the Inner Party members sip their wine, feast on private food, and toke on their designer drugs. We are all so quaint to you, after all, aren't we? Bring it on, Thornton. I may be turning 40, but I won't go out without a fight to the death!"

William's body was rigid, and his fists were balled up in front of him, ready to strike out at the MDP when they came for him. Instead, all he heard were a few laughs from his stoned fellow workers out in the audience. There was no arrest. Jack Thornton merely stooped down and brought his mouth to William's pulsing ear. William could smell the odor of fish as the Inner Party member of the Founding Socialist Youth whispered, "William, you will be called soon. We know how you can serve us now. I understand, my boy. It will happen soon, so you need not stress yourself much longer." This time, they weren't hovering in the air. The two MDP droids started to march out of the room, their jackboots striking the floor with loud thumps, and the music changed to Wagner's *Flight of the Valkyries*. William stepped gingerly off the riser, and watched, with his mouth agape, as Jack Thornton waved to the sleeping workers and strolled, on his leather Italian-made loafers, out of the restaurant.

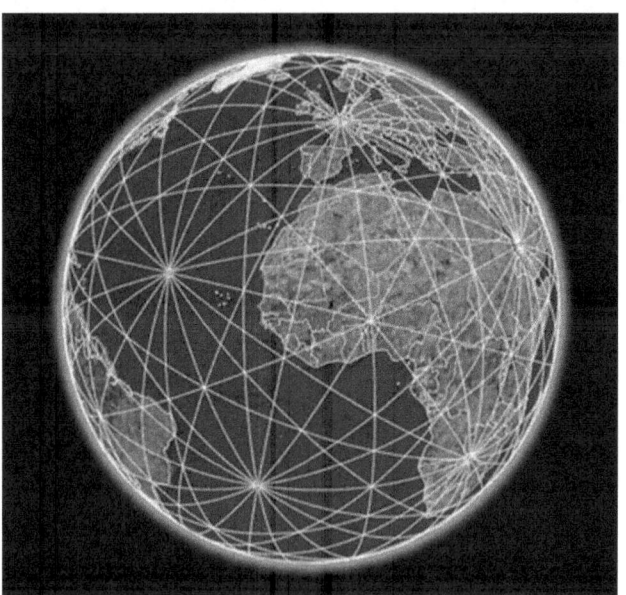

"Digital human body copies! I loved it!" Timothy said, as he walked with William back to their hostel. Ronda had met a woman she knew, and they decided to go watch the waves come in on the beach at La Jolla Shores.

"I suppose that's all you got out of my speech. Do you ever take anything seriously, Timothy?"

The young man's bisexual face frowned. "Of course I do, Willie! I told you about Roger, didn't I? If I was ever blocked, I *would* kill myself. It's the truth! How could I go on without my friends online, and the games we play, and the places we go together to enjoy ourselves? I love looking at people, touching them, and then storing them on my digital home. Which is my home? Is it online or is it in our hostel? I think I prefer online because I meet people there I would never meet at Minimind or in our hostel. We have such secret fun together! Don't you have a sex life, Willie? I've never seen you meet up with anyone. Are you a troll, or some kind of creepy eunuch?"

"Get out, Timothy! I've had enough of your meddling in my life for one night. You have no history of our race in that head of yours, do you? Didn't your parents ever teach you about the racism that existed in this country before Big Bro? I think it exists now, but people are too distracted by the media and the lies to see it. Did you ever wonder why you weren't paid during your internship? We get a pittance for what we do. Do you want to know why that is?"

Timothy sighed as he stood inside the doorway. "Shh! You will get us arrested with that kind of talk. You have never been really happy with your life, have you, William? I'm so sad for you, but I can't help you anymore. Tonight I heard you talk about things that made no sense. You must learn to go inside yourself and see who you are. Big Bro gives us the freedom to be ourselves—whatever your sexual desires may be—but if you don't take the time to go there, you will never see who your truly are. Get online and socialize. I have 15,000 followers on the Bro Channel, and my videos get millions of viewers. What do you do? Good night, Willie. Happy fortieth."

William closed the door after Timothy. All he wanted to do was get back to his diary, but he knew he only had one more spy camera deactivator chip left. He sat down on his cot and decided to think about what he would write in his diary once he had the time to invest. He was uncertain about what had happened at the restaurant. Was Jack Thornton playing cat and mouse with him? What did he really mean about calling for him? William supposed it was just a gentler way of telling him about the moment of his arrest and confinement or even about his execution. Or, perhaps his father was all wrong. Maybe he was senile and living in a kind of deluded fixation with the past. His father may be the one who lied to him about history because he never lived life outside of academia. William had never seen anybody arrested. It was all rumor and conjecture, as most of the Outer Party workers spent their days inside, working on the computers and other structures that controlled the droids and other automated systems. William had actually enjoyed many of his creative projects. Big Brother's home life was that of an intelligent surfer and lover of nature. But then, there was his sister, Ruth, and all that she had told him about the Ministry of Mindful Bliss.

At night. It always happened at night. William lay down on his cot, and the wall display of the Mindfulness

Network droned on with its programming. William never watched any shows—not even the ones he created. The inane subject matter and meaningless commercialism made his head ache. William closed his eyes and tried to concentrate. He found himself thinking about the woman he had met briefly from the Erotica and Romance section. There was something about her manner that both threatened and intrigued him. Timothy had perhaps hit upon a deeper trouble inside William's consciousness.

The dream he had was void of color, just the way his father said he and other citizens over 65 saw life. His mother, Rose, was being pushed in a wheelchair outside the Gerontology units by an android nurse. William was seeing all of this from a spy camera inside the drone hovering above them. His mother looked up and began to speak to the drone. William came down closer to Rose to hear what she was telling him.

"Save your father," she said clearly. "He needs you. Go to Ruth and Esther. They can help you."

His drone lifted up and began to speed away from the gerontology units and toward the dark Ministry of Freedom building. As he came toward it, William could see a pinpoint of light coming from one of the suites at the topmost level. His drone got closer, and the light gradually became brighter, larger and soon he could see the source of the light. Big Bro was standing at an open window with his arms outstretched, welcoming the drone back home. As William's drone came into the surrounding light, the radiant waves from Big Bro began to pulsate and glow even brighter until William realized it was a black hole of some kind, and William and his drone were getting sucked inside Big Brother's open mouth.

A vibrating, interconnected net was cast before him, and William could see sparkling points of light at each intersecting point on the net. As his drone got closer, the points of light expanded into a tapestry of blinking forms. Closer, they were both human and android, performing the thousands of jobs dictated under the umbrella of Big Bro. Above it all, the brain of Big Bro was flashing and igniting streams of digital signals out to the connections inside the net. It was all wrapped over the Earth's surface, and William could see the workers were located all around the world, on every continent and island. It was making William experience a peaceful glow of comfort, until the electronic net began to pulse and pound out a hellacious rhythm, crackling and lashing around like a whip, throwing droids and humans out into the ocean, crushing their bodies against buildings and mountains, until the complete network was destroyed.

William felt a figure behind him, and when his drone turned, the source of the destruction came into view. It was the figure of a huge black woman holding a laptop computer. Her face was familiar, but it kept changing form. First, she looked like his mother, Rose, and then she morphed into the woman from Erotica and Romance, and then, she became his sister, Ruth. Finally, the face of his niece, Esther, appeared. But behind her William saw the running form of Big Bro. He was armed with a laser rifle, and he was aiming it at the head of this woman.

"Watch out! Run!" William shouted, and then he awoke. The wall channel was broadcasting a droid preparing one of the latest recipes from Big Bro's kitchen, which was yet another soy and ramen concoction.

Part 2

Chapter One

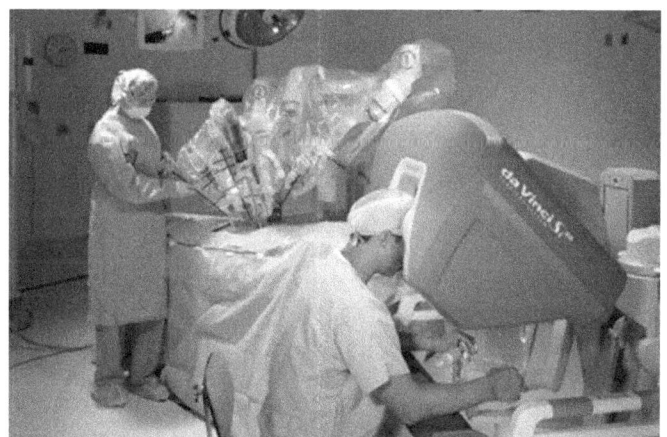

The second day closer to his fortieth birthday, William decided to follow his dream's dictates. His parents told him that dreams were very powerful instruments in the Bible and in other ancient texts. The tribal elders had always relied upon the interpreters of dreams to seek a way forward for the whole tribe. William wanted to follow his dream, so he ate a soy meal muffin and headed over to his sister's place of employment downtown. She worked as a computer programmer at the Ministry of Living Bliss on Sixth Avenue.

The same party slogans appeared on the face of Minibliss in flashing neon:

WAR IS IN THE PAST
FREEDOM IS ALWAYS TODAY
IGNORANCE IS IN WRITTEN HISTORY

Ruth worked on the sixth floor in the medical droid programming department. She was one of the main developers of code that took the latest medical technique and turned it into algorithms to be used by the androids out in the field at the variety of hospitals, clinics and gerontology centers. William had kept in contact with his sister by text messages, but she had devised a personal encryption method that even the Ministry of Freedom couldn't decipher. She was the first person to tell him about how the process of Mindful Bliss was actually a way to move under-performing humans quickly into a state of useless catatonia. The biggest discovery of the research department in her workplace had been that human genetic code could be programmed to break-down in order to serve the underhanded purposes of the government. Just as products on the market had been developed with the same programmed obsolescence, Big Bro could now do the same thing with humans who were losing their value to the system. Each droid and every human on the planet had brain implants that constantly monitored their mental and physical health, and when they began to break-down because of age, electronic malfunction, or disease, an immediate alert signal was sent to the Inner Party workers employed in the Ministry of Visual Reality, who were ready to initiate the "Mindful Bliss" implementation. William had purposefully not mentioned his knowledge of this secret during his impromptu argument with Thornton at the restaurant because he knew they would eventually connect it with his sister and her job at Minibliss.

William had come to visit his sister under the guise of obtaining his transference information. Every Outer Party member had to be indoctrinated with a collection of instructional implants aimed at assisting them through the "peaceful and rejuvenating process of elder transference." Depending on your value in society, citizens could be completely wiped from the grid of life, or they could, like his parents, be isolated inside the lonely confines of the gerontology units. He and his sister had developed a kind of spoken clandestine code to communicate about the issue of saving their parents from deactivation. After his father lost his teaching job and was moved to the Gerontology units, they believed it would only be a matter of weeks or days before Minibliss moved him completely off the grid together with Rose, their mother. *Perhaps this is why Jack Thornton is calling for me,* William thought, climbing the stairs to the sixth floor. He hated taking the powervators because they played the horrible music of Big Bro's favorites, which usually consisted of selections from the ancient songs of the Beach Boys, Jan and Dean, and the grand leader's personal favorite group, Dick Dale and the Del-Tones. If William heard "Miserlou" one more time, he was certain he would not have to be forced into a catatonic state by an implant, it would happen by musical bombardment.

Nobody, of course, knew Ruth was his sister. This was information that would be kept unknown until William was entered into the records at 40 years of age. Every human could remember his or her family and their lives together before they became Outer Party members, but their surnames were taken from them when they left the family to enter the Outer Party work apparatus of school and then employment. The family domicile was, in fact, destroyed after the children were raised and employed by Big Bro, and they were never allowed to live together as a family unit after that physical destruction took place. However, since every employed Outer Party member was without a family name for many years, the computer systems basically ignored your family status. This meant that family members, if they wished, and if they could find them, could visit each other at their respective hostels, places of employment, or even gerontology units, as long as they never mentioned their family relationship out loud. It was, to William, another one of the completely idiotic rules of the Inner Party, but it gave Big Bro and his controllers a way to fool Outer Party members into believing that their families were all reunited when and if they were able to reach the age of 40. It was one of Big Bro's biggest lies. The supposed state of Mindful Bliss that William and all others entered into at age 40 was also a supposed reunion with the biological family, and many of the reality programs created by Minimind were aimed at perpetrating and extending this lie.

His sister's back was to him as he entered the cubicle. She was moving images on the screen, deep in concentration, not even aware he was in the room.

"The two new characters on Big Bro's House Party Bash are being moved this week. Who do you think will take charge after they leave?" William's code was translated as "Mom and Dad are getting moved by Minibliss when I turn 40. How do we stop this?"

Ruth swiveled in her chair to face her brother. She was ten years younger, and her face had a radiant quality with high cheekbones and full lips. Even without make-up, she was a strikingly beautiful black woman. "Yes, I love that show! I think Bing and Babs are perfect, but they'll need to be given the right equipment to survive the Party Purges. Are you here to receive your instructional implants, William?" This code translated into "We need to give Mom and Dad tracking implants so we can follow their movements."

As William sat under the glaring lights, Ruth pushed the memory chip into one of the five slots on the back of William's neck. They were put there by the Ministry of Visual Reality when he turned 18 and graduated from college. They made it easy for each ministry to add whatever information or instructions the Outer Party members needed to follow. All William had to do after receiving his chip was place his palm on any telescreen monitor, such as the one in his hostel room. The screen would immediately fill with the menu listing the contents of the chip so he could view it. However, William knew that his sister would also be inserting two extra chips into his slots. These were the tracking implants that William would be using to insert into his parents' memory slots in order to follow them.

After he left Minibliss, his sister immediately got on her phone and texted him with their encrypted symbols. William was getting on the YSW tram on Broadway to take him back to Old Town when he got her first message. He sat in a seat next to a young party member with red eyes. The lad was obviously stoned from THC and listening to music through his ear buds. William pushed the decrypt button, which Ruth had created just for their two phones. Ruth said that Inner Party Members had the same technology, but she had created their encryption language just for personal communications. The words showed clearly on his screen:

It's begun. After you put the tracking chips into them, you will be introduced to her. She's part of our group, so don't go hurting her. Are you still going to try to penetrate the Inner Party? I thought we were going to get Mom and Dad out of San Diego and start a revolt with the transmissions we've stolen over the years.

William responded to Ruth as quickly as his fingers could press the keys on his phone.

You told me you could remotely deactivate the spy cameras. If we can do that I know we can get inside the Minifree building. I want proof that there are no people of color in the Inner Party. Dad said that when the revolt began against the droids taking jobs from humans, the young socialists saw that blacks and other people of color were fighting back in greater numbers. We didn't believe all the propaganda about free drugs and sex. Most of our jobs were being taken by those robots, and we knew it was just another racist attempt to divide our people by luring us into the fold with tempting distractions. I want to show that Big Bro is not only killing off the old and feeble, but he's also keeping people of color out of the Inner Party. I know it might not mean much to blacks like Timothy, who have already sold out, but there are many of us who will fight against this kind of discrimination just the way we did during the Civil Rights days Dad and Mom always told us about.

The kid next to William turned toward him and grinned. William remembered one of Karl Marx's comments about religion being the opiate of the people. No, drugs were the key ingredient to oppress the people in the society of Big Bro. His sister's response came back as the YSW tram turned the corner onto Old Town Avenue.

All right, William. I'll help you get in there. But I'm going to get our group ready for a back-up plan in case we don't come out of there. I don't think it's worth proving they're a bunch of racists. Isn't it evil enough to kill off the population by monitoring their health and intelligence? Who cares who's in the Inner Party? It's what they do to all of us outside that really matters!

As he walked toward his hostel, the marine layer began to cover the land again, and William's mind floated up into it. He could feel the misty fog on his face. His life as a child with his sister, Ruth, had been typical for families after the Revolution of 2028. Each family was given the same type of house, a one-story, two-bedroom wooden structure that was outfitted with the latest computer, telescreen and online gear. However, this place was not allowed to be a home, which was what his parents had described to them in the secret language they had devised to circumvent the spy cameras. William still recalled the way he and Ruth would hurry into their bedroom to run what his parents had said through their decryption software. They had never shared this method of family communications with any other families, as it would have meant an immediate arrest of all of them. The words were what came back to William over the years, as he labored for Big Bro, and they were what sustained him as he approached his fortieth birthday one day from now. He never really knew who had exactly said the words, as they came out deciphered all together, without quotations or even punctuation marks. It wasn't until this week, when William decided to start his written diary that his father's words were put down as recorded fact. Until this week, William's mind simply let the words flow through his mind, the way they were doing now, and they served as a strange antidote to the constant media propaganda coming at him from Big Bro.

We had a farm where we could grow our own vegetables and nobody told us how much to sell or how much to give back to the state it was all ours to do with as we saw fit the chickens were in the yard where I played and I watched the big roosters guard the hens calling out a secret squawking signal when a hawk flew over and the hens all knew to race into the coops and take cover and my father showed me my chores to do like milking cows with my hands holding the teats red and wrinkled and oh so soft against my palm and squeezing grasping the top of the teat by wrapping my thumb and forefinger around it then compressing the teat and wrapping my other fingers around it and as I squeeze this forces milk already in the teat out in a stream without sliding my hand up and down the teat releasing the compression without fully letting go of the teat this allows more milk to drop from the udder into the teat so I can compress my fingers from top to bottom and squeeze out the milk because if my hand isn't sliding on the teat it reduces the chance of irritation to the cow and we love and always learn from our animals as they give us sustenance and what we eat on our table as a family we can pray to God for our next day's meal without losing sight of the hawks in life but they come and my father told me before he owned the farm we had no property we worked the land for the white owners and they paid us to do the work until Civil Rights came and this was our saving grace this was our chance to own land and to raise our own corn our own cows our own chickens but then when I married and took over the farm there came a new movement with new rights for Big Bro we became teachers and left the farm because the droids had taken over but we fought them in college and people came out into the street to fight the droid keepers and the computer young people who had gradually taken over academia with their multiple-choice tests and their obliteration of reading and literature until all was a visual experience a monotonous stream of color action movement excitement and free love with drugs and sex and there was blood in the streets like in the days of Civil Rights and anti-war they told everybody it was all for anti-war because the war had become the old men's game and would no longer exist in the new plan of Big Bro and his young socialists the socialists for free expression and peace and libertarian values not the communist totalitarianism but freedom and always and eternally now but we fought them and the poor blacks and other people of color who had been kept in prisons became fighters with us against these young socialists but they were too much and they hacked with their computers into the banks businesses government databases all over the world it happened and soon there became the new age of computers droids drones and spy cameras that have stolen cultures and languages and made them mockeries of civilization and you children know the rest because we live in it to this day but listen to us when we tell you it wasn't like that before 2028 we learned to keep books to record history and written facts of what we saw became fair laws and civil rights not visual spying on everyone the way it is now the way they lie to you and say it's to keep you safe that was the way they tricked us with the patriot act and other secret spying on us for our own good for our own protection and the young socialists were able to turn it all around and make it seem like they had stopped the warmongers the old men who ran the country and spied on us from their computers but now Big Bro owns the devices and he makes the visual rules and we suffer and our home is now a house and you will be taken from us one day to go into the YSW school and then out to work in the ministries of fear and dictatorship that they lie about and make up their rules as they go and tell you it's all for your own good but we can never give up and you now know the truth and you will never forget it until you turn 40 when the final lie will take you away from us forever oh God let us pray for help and pray for the animals and the land that has been stolen from us and given to the Inner Party and the secret wealth of the young libertines who live in a world of debauchery and fraud.

William opened the door to his room, and his head was filled with the words from his youth. This was why he wanted to write it all down and preserve it in a record. As it was, it was like the never ending raving of a mad man. Where was this eternal now with its computerized and drone-spying reality really going? William now believed it was going straight to Hell. He collapsed on his cot as the telescreen on the wall kept up its incessant lying about living a healthier life and enjoying sexier programs with the latest music and best women and the most exciting sports imaginable, and for harvesting from nature using the most advanced technology in the history of the world. Big Bro's handsome face came into full screen, and William heard his master's voice just before he fell into a deep sleep:

"Stop Dr. Drury and his book before he becomes a threat to our world peace!"

Chapter Two

O·n this, the day before he turned 40, William awoke to the sound of a siren. Other years, this was the signal to warn of an approaching hurricane or earthquake, since the process of oil extraction during the years before the revolution had made our world, according to Big Bro, "a constantly dangerous natural disaster." This was why there were daily ads on the telescreens announcing the latest plan to conserve energy or to save water or to prevent forest fires. Since most citizens never left their work places to see what was left of the natural habitat, they had to rely on the reports by the Ministry of Mindfulness. William, having worked at Minimind since he was 21, knew these reports were compiled using old video footage from days past when the land and farms were fertile and bountiful, and humans worked to keep the natural habitat safe and the farms abundant, but the actual truth was something to be speculated by Outer Party members huddled together inside storm centers, when these sirens went off. Of course, nobody dare speak what he or she was thinking about the state of the environment because any kind of collective thinking out loud about any topic, including the weather, was subject to a visit from the MDP droids.

William pulled on his Minimind overalls and grabbed a soy muffin as he headed out the door to the storm shelter on Old Town Avenue. The misty marine layer was there, but there were no storm clouds or funnels forming, so William thought the siren might be another ploy to get members out of their hostels so the droids could go in to inspect the premises while they were at the storm shelters. At this thought, William turned around, ran back to his hostel room and retrieved his black diary from under the mattress. He clutched it to his heart as he raced down the street, along with hundreds of others, until he could see the entrance to the shelter about one hundred yards ahead.

"Brother, follow me," a female voice whispered, and William felt his arm being yanked sideways. It was the black woman from the Erotica and Romance Department. She pulled him away from the shelter entrance and toward the Casa de Pico Restaurant where the party had been given for him the night before.

William kept looking up in the air for any surveillance drones as he was pulled into the back entrance of the restaurant by this woman who moved swiftly, her legs powerfully dodging bus carts and tables, until they were standing inside the same back room where William's 40th transference party was held. Today, they were the only ones there, as the entire restaurant had cleared out after the siren sounded. The woman's dark eyes riveted on William. "Don't worry. One of our members will be in the storm shelter. He's instructed to mark us present and accounted for. I want to talk to you about your father and his book. My name is Leila, but in our group I'm known as Judith."

"What group? How do you know my father? This book. My father never wrote such a book."

"The Authority is our group's name. I know your father because he is our group's leader. Yes, he has written this book. He has also written many more books that have never been discovered by Big Bro. This was the first one that has surfaced to be connected to him. I want you to know that you and your family have been watched and protected for many years. Now it is time to establish the authority of the people once more." The woman's voice was loud and strong.

"Why are you telling me all this?" William's eyes

scanned the walls for spy cameras.

"There are none. This is a safe zone. We have many of these meeting places throughout the world. We are ready to bring the living truth to light, and we want you to be with us when we establish our authority." Leila or Judith took William's hands into her own. He didn't know if he were dealing with some kind of mad woman, and he expected they would be arrested at any moment.

"How do you know the truth any more than my father? He's been trapped in academia, and I've been slaving along with you inside Minimind. The only truth I know is what my parents told me when I was a child. I could never explain what they said because we could never write things down. What do you mean about my father writing books for you? What's in those books, and why did you make him your leader?"

"Most of us could never risk coming out until we were ready. John, your father, explains it as if we were new plants that have been hibernating beneath the soil for years, taking in the full power of Mother Earth, evolving our methods and making our secret plans. 'When the sunlight of truth comes, you will all arise and take your rightful places among all free peoples,' he told us. Today, William, I am here to tell you that as his son, you are to be next in command. But first, we must ask that you give us your encryption technology to use in our group. John has told us about it, and this was one of the main reasons why he became our leader. He said you have it, as does your sister, Ruth, and she has already told you about my meeting with you, correct?" Her thick eyebrows arched up, and she licked her full, red lips. William felt sexually aroused for the first time in many months.

"This is all going too fast. How many of you are there, and what are you planning? How can I trust you are telling me the truth?"

Judith took a memory chip from her Minimind jacket pocket and held it out. "Turn around, and I'll show you," she said.

William felt her slide the chip into one of the slots in the back of his neck.

"When you get back to your room, I want you to use your last spy camera deactivation chip and watch what's on this memory chip," she instructed him. "It will explain everything you want to know about our group and how your father became our leader. It will also explain why those books are so important to what we're doing now. Tomorrow, as you are going through the 40 transference, we will all be communicating to set our plan into action. Our plan is also on the chip. Now. Are you ready to give me the cryptography phone in your pocket?" Judith extended her hand.

William took a deep breath. Ruth had told him to expect a visit from this woman, and now she was here. He also knew from his sister that there were others who were part of the revolt. He realized that it was all about to happen, and he was filled with a mixture of excited anticipation and fearful dread. It was like entering a pitch-dark maze without any map. He slowly took his phone from his jacket pocket. He held onto it for a minute, staring deeply into this woman's brown eyes. The entire future of his family was at stake, and he was turning over their technological secret to someone he did not know. What if she were a spy? What if the MDP came rushing in at the exact moment he handed her his phone? He extended his phone, and she took it!

"Thank you, brother. We must get back before the all clear siren sounds. The droids should be about finished with the inspection of hostels by now. We could falsify the roll call, but then they run the DNA check. Let's go!"

William wanted to hug her, or at least thank her for being part of his family's escape plans, but she was now running out of the restaurant at full speed, and this woman could really run. William took off after her, nearly tripping over the same riser he had spoken from when confronting Jack Thornton the night before. He was more anxious to return to his hostel room than he had been for the nineteen years he had worked at the Ministry of Mindfulness.

The droids had inspected his hostel room. Some of his clothes hanging in the small closet had been moved, and his cot mattress was curled up, exposing the underlying piston supports. William headed directly for the telescreen on the wall behind his bed. He first took out the spy camera deactivator chip, turned it into the on position, and watched the red light on the camera suspended from the ceiling in the center of his room slowly fade out. He then took out the two tracking chips from the slots behind his neck, which would later be inserted into his father and mother in order to determine where they would be taken by Minibliss. Finally, William placed his right palm on the telescreen's surface, and the menus from his memory chips came into view. There were the instructions his sister had given him about the 40 Transference Process that was taking place tomorrow. But it was the second chip he wanted to view first. The first menu item said "History of The Authority." The second menu item said "Our Leader, Dr. John Alfred Drury." The last menu item said "The Plan."

William touched the first menu title with his right index finger. The letters dissolved to bring up a video that showed a drone sitting on a table inside one of the thousands of offices at the Ministry of Mindfulness. The black woman from Erotica and Romance, Leila or Judith, came into view and faced the camera. Her hand reached over and touched the silver, two-foot wide unmanned aerial vehicle. It was obviously one of Big Bro's drones, as the Minimind logo was still on the sides of the fuselage. The logo had the face of Big Bro and the letters "Ministry of Mindfulness" printed around his portrait.

"Welcome. My name is Judith Watimba, and I am a proud member of The Authority. What I have here is one of the millions of drones that you see spying all over our campus pod, and it is going to show you what Big Bro never lets you see. One of the first actions we took as an organization was to steal one of these drones, and change its configuration, so it would work on our behalf. I am now going to use this drone to show you scenes of what your government has never shown you before. These scenes will serve as the driving purpose behind The Authority, and I will also explain our history by alluding to our movement and how it began by sending out just a single embezzled UAV aircraft."

The camera panned to the left and showed the control panel for the drone and the person seated behind it. "This is Robert Fowler. He will be directing the flight of our touring drone. We have many trained operators around the world in The Authority. They serve as our recorders of truth to combat the big lies of Big Bro."

William bit on his lower lip and looked around the room. He expected an intrusion by the MDP at any second. What was he doing watching this secret video by some amateur group of rebels? Did they really expect to overthrow Big Bro with one stolen drone?

The drone rose up inside the room, hovered as the pilot tested his controls, and then shot out the window into the San Diego streets. "We'll first see how droids have taken over most of the work. When Dr. Drury told us in his first book, *Unions*, how humans used to be employed at these jobs, and they made a good living for their families because of their unions, we had no frame of reference. We had been raised seeing the videos of all the humans working at the factories, schools, stores, farms and markets, and we believed we in the ministries were serving them. Now, look, brothers and sisters, as our drone goes inside this factory. See those assembly lines and packing stations? They are all robots doing the jobs we thought were all done by humans."

William watched the mechanical arms of the robot put together the drone with lightning precise movements, fitting the parts together in seconds. It would have taken a human at least an hour to do such detailed assembly.

"Unions were no longer needed because there were no humans to do the work. In the past, before the Revolt against Robots in 2028, the owners told the citizens there would be better, higher-paying jobs created to run these robots, so there was no threat to human employment. As you can see, there are no humans running these robots. They are all controlled remotely by the Inner Party inside offices on the top floors of the Ministry of Visual Reality. No Outer Party member is allowed to see what you are viewing now. In book two of Dr. Drury's opus, *Robots*, he explains how Big Bro used the evolution of these droids to fight the owners and take-over the world."

These books were never mentioned to William. His father must have been secretly writing them while William was working for Big Bro. However, if he could read them, perhaps it would connect a lot of the memories he had that made no sense to him up to this point.

"Now we will go out to the agricultural world of Big Bro. From this height, you might assume this was a conventional farm with the farmer and his family and his hired help working to till the soil, plant the crops and harvest them when the time comes. However, watch closely, as we come down to get a better look. These rows are dug by remotely controlled droids driving the tractors. That's why they're so perfectly aligned and manicured so well. There is not a single human on this farm, and the intelligence of the programmed droids is sufficient to run all the work that needs to be done. Since most of the Outer Party eats generally soy-based products, one wonders where all these tomatoes, potatoes, corn and other produce go. Dr. Drury says it's sold to other Inner Party members in other countries."

This was not new to William, as he was aware of the hording of food and other special items by the Inner Party. It was his father's relationship to The Authority that made him uncomfortable. All of this involvement would mean certain death as a traitor to Big Bro. The plan they have must be a good one, or else all of this secret information will have been obtained for nothing.

"We can assume that the work is being done by droids, so this is why humans have become expendable. Dr. Drury's final book, the book that was discovered by Big Bro, says that the final plan by Big Bro is to create a world kept by an exclusive group of Inner Party members and their outer slaves. In *The Insane Call Us Free*, Dr. Drury speculates that the Inner Party is creating a political system that is invoking a way to eliminate entire populations and replace them with remotely controlled droids. Not only does this solve the over-population problem, it also allows Big Bro to use its computer and spy technology to monitor the health and performance of humans in the Outer party. Dr. Drury said there was a mad man in the 1940s who wanted to control humanity in this way, and he was also trying to annihilate whole populations of unacceptable humans. His name was Adolph Hitler and what he did was kill millions in the name of cleansing the races. Big Bro is also doing this, but with much wider and more profound consequences. The 40 Transference is a process by which the world's population is being filtered to extinction; all the while we are being lied to over these digital networks that these elders of ours are living a life of eternal bliss. Dr. Drury also said that this type of thinking began way back in the early Twenty-first Century when governments were controlled for the best interests of corporations and the rich in a system called government lobbying. They also privatized the military in what was then the United States of America in order to fight proxy wars to develop even more fossil fuel energy to feed the coffers of these rich few. For example, the gun lobby, as it was called back then, was a group of mostly men who allowed the free sale and distribution of weapons, which in turn eliminated thousands of citizens a year through murders, suicides, and accidental deaths. When the revolution was won by Big Bro in 2028, we were told they took control from these old men, who were warmongers and industrialists, and now we were living in constant peace. At what cost do we maintain this peace, and who will need to die to maintain control by another, much more dangerous minority of Inner Party leaders?"

What peace can there be when spy cameras and drones watch and listen to your every move? William thought. *What weapons do we have to protect ourselves against the peacekeepers? We in the Outer Party work so much we never have time to have a life off the digital grid. Even when we do, there are so many places off limits that we might as well be prisoners like those people of color mentioned in the video and by my father in his books. The biggest lie is that they tell us we are free. The prisons have moved into the streets of our cities.*

As the drone flew back inside the office window at the Ministry of Living Bliss, the voice of Judith Watimba concluded. "The Authority grew out of these revelations and the books of Dr. Drury. We hope you can now play a part in our quest to take back our heritage, stop the hidden holocaust, and make the people the real authority in our world!"

William was anxious to see the second menu item, "Our Leader, Dr. John Alfred Drury." He pushed the button and another video appeared. This time, William was watching his father speaking into the camera from his college classroom. As he spoke, he did his usual pacing routine around the room, just the way he had done at home. He also kept adjusting his glasses and thrusting them at the camera when he was making an especially important point. He was younger in this video, probably in his early sixties, as his black cotton hair was just beginning to turn white, and his voice had the vigor William remembered from him during his frequent lectures to the family.

"Once the means of production have been taken over, the only method of revolution becomes a plan to reverse-engineer the system in place and use the technology of the adversary against himself. Big Bro's comrades were able to do this in the beginning, when they used computer and robotic technologies to steal the wealth of the developed nations. The remaining poorer countries, as a result, quickly fell into line. When I was young, the developed nations were fighting over the natural resources to support both the technological innovations and the fossil fuel system of energy. Lip service was paid to developing alternative forms of energy, but the reality of the so-called 'War on Terror' showed that the actual battle was being waged against those countries controlling the most possibilities for more oil and mineral development. Wars became proxy conflicts, wherein the huge industrialized countries like China and the United States, as they were called then, supplied the 'revolutionaries' with the weapons and technology necessary to fight the terrorists *de jour*."

William had heard most of this, although his father's voice seemed to take a more passionate tone in this video. It was almost as if he were auditioning for a leadership role in the organization.

"Big Bro was able to overcome the unions by convincing the white collar workers that they were serving the factories, farms and stores as well as the human workers who had thriving occupations overseeing the technology that ran them. Now, with our new intelligence, we can now see that there is no need for humans in most of these jobs and that BB needed a plan to keep the economy moving without wars to give it momentum. The specialized robots and computerized economy gave them the door to access the answer to this dilemma. As a cover, they kept filling the workers with the lies on the digital network. The Outer Party workers in the ministries believed there were humans out there they were serving. In fact, the working population had been completely replaced by computerized droids. All the recreation was controlled also. The former National Parks became controlled tree museums where there are just as many drones, droids and spy cameras all around as there are in the cities. The free sex and drugs were bribes to keep the younger population happy. The population, of course, was getting younger by the day because of the final plan to get rid of anybody who had become older, sicker or who were judged to be in any way not serving the best interests of the Inner Party's needs."

His father's pacing was getting faster, and his tone held more gravitas. He was obviously ready to make his pitch for becoming the leader. He thrust his glasses toward the camera before he spoke.

"If you want to save what is left of humanity, then you must make a choice to rise up and fight this system. There is an Achilles' heel. Big Bro has gotten too greedy. Their systems rely on remote control and Wi-Fi too much, and if you can penetrate this system to first deactivate the drones and the spy cameras, then you will be free to take back what is rightfully yours by invading the Ministry of Freedom and becoming weaponized. The longer you wait, my friends, the tighter the noose will become around your necks. I was born, I believe, in 1984, but when I reached 40, I became a creature of bliss. I was able to counteract the implant they gave me with the help of some of my enterprising students. In four years, when I reach 65, I will be marked for destruction, and my wife, God bless her soul, has already been locked inside the Gerontology Units with these blasted droid nannies whirring all around her. I wish you could see it! Every sneeze, drool, defecation and demented vision is cared for in seconds, as these inhuman droids do their work to clean things up on the surface, but nothing is ever said about her inner world, her desperate need for love and affection, and the warmth of other humans touching her and giving her a reason to go on. If I become your leader, I will return you to the authentic family life you deserve. The elderly and infirm need not be destroyed for the economic advantage of the Inner Party. Peace is good, but it comes at the cost of our sanity. The totalitarian control of our loved ones and the daily media bombardments, free sex, and drug-induced happiness have made this a prison on Earth. They have divided us, and we are all prisoners awaiting our executioners. Will you let me help you rescue humanity before we all become victims of Capital Punishment? I am willing to risk it all to help you."

William became frightened about viewing the final menu item. It was obvious that this "Plan" involved him, as this group had recruited his father, John, as their leader, and now he was being sucked into the scheme like a prize winner on a Big Bro Network game show. He thought about texting his sister, but then he remembered he had given his phone to Leila/Judith. Again, the thought of this all being a trap of some kind came to him. Whether he joined them or didn't join them, Big Bro would get him in the end. That was the nature of life in 2050, and William was, at heart, a pessimist. However, as he had nothing better to do at the moment, he pressed the button for "The Plan."

This time, there was no video that came up on his wall's telescreen. Instead, a notice first appeared saying, "This information will self-destruct after viewing. The Authority." William, also, it seemed, was not trusted.

Then, text came rolling across the screen like one of Big Bro's banners: *1. Upload virus into Ministries. 2. Stage riot to bring out the MDP. 3. Confiscate weapons from the Ministry of Freedom. 4. Invade the Inner Party offices and return control to The Authority. 5. Return the power to the people and to their families.*

The screen dissolved into a pinpoint of light. When William saw that the chip he inserted into the port on the telescreen had begun to smoke, he quickly popped it out. He gingerly scooped the chip into his hand, but it was so hot he dropped it onto the floor. He watched, with rapt attention, as it began to liquefy into a puddle of heated metal at his feet.

Chapter Three

ater that evening, William heard a knock at his door. A mini-droid stood there on the threshold staring up at him. These little buggers were used mostly to do jobs like street sweeping and emptying the trash. Their intelligence was very low, yet they still had a voice synthesizer, and this one began speaking to him. His LED eyes sparkled, and his titanium arm reached out to him with wiggling fingers.

"Come, William. I will take you where you are wanted. Right now. It can't wait."

On the telescreen, an ad for a new designer drug to increase study skill attention and job concentration was being shown. A young man wearing Minimind overalls was running faster than an MDP robot who was, in turn, chasing down a fleeing thief. "Get a head start on the competition," the voice-over said.

The little machine led William down a back alley near the Plaza next to the Visitor Center. The droid motioned toward two wooden doors on what looked like an old wine cellar in the ground next to the building. "Open," he said.

William pulled on both of the steel rings, and the two doors spread apart revealing several steps down into the darkness. The little robot climbed down before him, and William followed. When he reached the bottom, an odor of wine casks, dust, and fermented grapes permeated the air in the darkness. "Who's there?" William asked.

The little droid pulled down the two doors behind them, which closed them inside like a tomb. When the lights came on, William saw they were big candles being lit by Leila or Judith, his colleague at Minimind. There were about ten of these foot-tall candles of blue, green, yellow and red, and as the woman lit each one, she turned to smile at William, her white teeth and dimpled smile flashing in the shadows like beacons from a world he had not visited in many years. In fact, the last time he had been with a woman of her beauty had been in college, and this was a marijuana-fueled tryst that was followed by a feast of junk food. The sex had been fast and furious, and there was no close relationship that followed. William knew that this woman was a mature and intelligent revolutionary who had been watching him for longer than he knew.

When they both sat down on two small stools next to one of the casks, she poured the wine from the spigot into goblets, and not wine glasses, and William was reminded of Shakespeare, for some reason. Was he playing the role of Othello to her Desdemona? Of course, Desdemona was a white Italian noble woman, and Othello was a Moorish General in Venice. Their marriage was doomed because of Othello's jealousy and Iago's treachery. Was William being enticed by this forbidden woman from the Erotica and Romance Department, where Big Bro created the romantic formulas for all those frustrated young people to devour like candy inside their lonely hostels? Was this all a temptation leading to his eventual doom?

"This little droid was also captured for our use. I'm happy you were able to come. William, I want to make a toast to you and to your brave father, John. Tomorrow, you will inherit his name, and, if all goes well, you will also be part of a new world of freedoms based on the family structure and the proper application of technology to serve all races and ages of humans. No longer will we lose our dignity under the thumb of Big Bro. In fact, if we can complete our plan, we may arrest this prison warden and put him on trial for crimes against humanity."

"How did you find out about my father and his books? I'm his son, and I never knew he had written them."

"I was in one of your father's classes. It was before they stopped offering that course to students, and I was fascinated by your father's way of explaining the variety of literature and poetry we covered. When he talked about books in their printed form, it was if he were discussing a lost child or close relative. The basic philosophical core of our movement came from his classes." Judith sipped from her wine goblet as she stared into the flame on one of the candles.

"I understand, but how did you get him to share the books? Did he know you were starting this group?" William took a long drink and savored the calm rivulets of numbness filling his brain with endorphins. It was quite a welcome change from the narcissistic hallucination of Big Bro weed.

Judith moved her eyes from the flame to his eyes and smiled. "I have no family. My parents were both killed during the Revolt against Robots. I was placed directly into a supervised youth hostel, and I learned the propaganda from the government on a daily basis. We were told world peace had finally been won, thanks to Big Bro and his cadre of young hackers and revolutionaries, and now a system of benevolent control would be initiated. We were shown videos of happy workers in the factories, farms, and stores, who were overseeing the labor of the droids. We now know these were all fictitious stories, as the droids had taken over, and my parents had lost their lives in vain. After I sent the stolen drone out to see what was really happening inside those buildings and on those farms, I wanted to kill Big Bro with my own hands. I was still in school, so it was I who approached your father about our group. I must say, he wasn't overjoyed."

"I agree. I have watched your videos, but what makes you believe you'll be able to overthrow an organization that was able to successfully hack into all the world's computer systems, disarm all the world's weapons of mass destruction, and control all the world's populations? My big concern is this. If they can disarm these weapons, then what will stop them from rearming them when threatened?"

Judith stood up and walked slowly over to William. She held her wine goblet aloft, as if it were a flag. Her tall and shapely young body sent a shiver of lust running through William's body.

"Long live the digital gods! William, we believe they will never use these weapons because they placed all their trust in computers and android technology. Your father says that the ability to create nuclear weapons became so dangerously common that all the weapons were destroyed, along with the written plans to assemble them. When Big Bro first came to power after 2028, his group's members were very idealistic, and they truly believed they could establish peace on Earth by destroying the very weapons that had caused such turmoil amongst developed nations. Do we have concrete evidence that all weapons of mass destruction were destroyed? No, we don't, but nobody in our group around the world has ever seen these weapons or has seen proof that they exist."

"But, again, none of you is in the Inner Party. I suggest we attempt to get access into this domain before we try any revolt. I think I know someone who might be approachable. Let me try this tomorrow, and then I'll let you know what I find out."

"Who is this person? What makes you think he might help us?"

"I've watched him for many years in my department at Minimind. He shows a certain friendliness and defiant attitude that I have never seen in any other Inner Party member. His name is Jack Thornton."

Judith smiled. "Oh yes! I know Mr. Thornton. He hired me, and he showed a great concern about my family having died in the revolution. He told me a day was coming when we humans would be getting our revenge against this take-over by droids. It really surprised me, as this kind of statement bordered upon sedition."

"That's why I want to approach him. He's young, but he seems to have empathy for the plight of Outer Party workers. With a sympathizer on the inside, we can make a lot more progress, don't you agree?" William felt like a child playing some kind of spy game. As an adult about to turn 40, however, he was thinking about the useless energy being expended. Big Bro was here for all time and would be ready for any revolt by the Outer Party. That's was the Ministry of Freedom was for. That's what William was really feeling. But life was standing still, and this woman was right in front of him. He brought the goblet to his lips and finished the wine in a single gulp.

Chapter Four

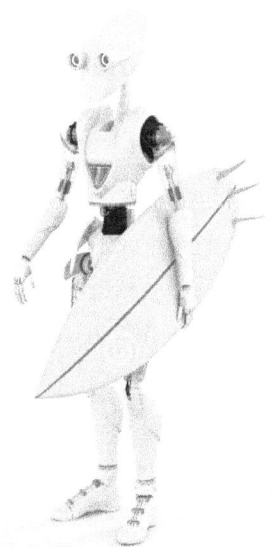

On the day he turned 40, William did not have to approach Jack Thornton because Jack Thornton approached him. Not only was William planning to visit the home of the Inner Party member, he was also attempting to recruit him to be an inside conspirator with The Authority. Unlike the little streetcleaner droid that Judith had sent, Thornton's droid was the latest model of home servant, and it looked quite human when William answered the door.

"William, my master has instructed me to escort you to his home. I believe he informed you of this visit, correct?" The droid looked like a surfer, with stringy-blond hair, flowered shorts, and a red tee with Big Bro's face on the front. He also wore the flip-flops of a bygone era before the revolution. William supposed this was Thornton's sense of humor being played out for all to see.

The droid drove a solar-powered hover craft that was painted red and blue, the colors of the San Diego Volts, the competitive surfing team owned by Big Bro. When they entered the gated community in the La Jolla Hills, William found himself gawking in awe at the luxurious architecture of the homes of Inner Party members. This was obviously where the profit went from the labors of the Outer Party. Gushing waterfalls, manicured lawns with gardens, trellises of roses, and hundreds of droids doing all the work. In addition, there were the ever-present Big Bro telescreens and drones to monitor every second of the eternal now.

The surfer droid inserted the security chip into the back of William's neck to allow him access. The door was opened to a wide foyer, and William followed the droid in. Inside, the furnishings were a combination of a Zen-like simplicity and the nature-loving posters of a surfer. Orange and black seemed to be the primary colors, with orange vases, walls, and sculptures and black wall trim, sofas, tables and chairs. The posters were holographic portraits of all the great surfing spots around the world: Superbank in Australia, Pipeline in Hawaii, Tofino in Canada and Les Cavaliers in France. Of course, there was also the smiling surfer persona of Big Bro.

William found it interesting that all the Inner Party homes were single-story units, just like the hostels and other buildings. Only the ministries were allowed to build the skyscrapers, and the elite members had to also obey this law. In the living room, Jack Thornton was standing in the center talking to a woman whose back was to William. As he approached the two, the woman turned. It was Leila from Erotica and Romance. She smiled broadly at her colleague, but she quickly turned back to face her boss, who was obviously in the middle of a speech of some kind.

Thornton was also wearing surfer attire, like his droid, except that his tee had a photo of Big Bro with a line drawn through his encircled face. *Where were the spy cameras? How does Thornton get away with being so blatantly disrespectful?* William thought. The increasing absurdity of this situation was difficult to comprehend.

"Willie! Glad you could make it. I was just explaining to Judith that The Authority was ready to initiate its plan as soon as I get the leadership mantle ready for your father. Without somebody filling the void left by Big Bro, we risk chaos in the streets and a possible counter-revolt. Judith was telling me you never knew your father had been recruited and was writing the books that would lay the foundation for the rebellion. Is this true?"

William shuffled his feet and looked down at them. He raised his head and looked into Thornton's blue eyes. "You call this secrecy? I thought my family was rebelling alone. We had our encrypted cell phone communications, and now The Authority has them. We had my father taking care of my mother in the Gerontology Units, and now he must lead this mighty revolution. No, I was not aware of any of this happening. So, there really is a Big Bro? I thought he was something you folks in the Inner Party created to keep us off the streets."

Thornton chuckled. "See? When you reach 40 the sense of humor gets better. With youth, it's all sarcasm. My comrades believe it's all downhill after 40, and this is the main reason I want to help you in your rebellion. I'm afraid that even though they have established world peace in our time, they are now taking themselves too seriously. There is no such thing as a perfect society based on maximizing pleasure and minimizing pain. This was the old philosophy of the Epicures, Hedonists and, much later, the Libertarians. Sadly, with each new generation, a specific way of looking at the world becomes fresh and startling to these new creatures on the planet. Like you, William, I had a father who taught history in the traditional manner. We always learned that history was written by the victors. The Young Socialists were victorious over their elders in a way that the Communists before them had never dreamed was possible. We literally stole the industrialized countries from under their technological noses. So, do you want to know how that was accomplished and how the YSW can be defeated?"

Both William and Judith nodded their heads.

"It actually began with the legalization of recreational marijuana in 2018, ten years before the Revolt against Robots wherein your parents gave their lives, Judith. The youth of the world became a much more consolidated force. They were angry with the way the world was being run by their elders, and they felt exploited in the technology sector with the variety of competitions for cheap labor such as internships, insourcing and outsourcing. It all reached a tipping-point when these young hot-heads began to believe they could shut-down the world's computer and energy systems from within, and then they could shut-down the weapons systems just as easily once they got the codes. As you all know, many hundreds of thousands of lives were lost in this 2028 revolt that began as a movement against technological droids and ended with the undercover theft of the entire developed world. It all happened because greed seems to be a possible ingredient in all human endeavors, and these new socialists were no different than any other revolutionary movement to come before."

William raised his hand, and Jack nodded.

"My father believed the Young Socialists put too much faith in their own technological genius. He said they never understood that youth is not able to be generous unless it is tamed by sickness and old age. When the supposed weaknesses in society are eliminated, what's left? A population like your Inner Party, which has an irrational fear of what makes us all human."

Jack waved his hand, and his droid left the room. "Little processors have big ears. Even though he's secure, I don't want any record of this to continue. At any rate, I will be erasing his memory chip when you leave. Please continue, William. What, pray tell, makes us all human?"

"Compassion. My father loves that word because it has such ancient roots. It means a sympathetic consciousness of others' distress together with a desire to alleviate it. Most of the old religions had this concept as its basis of thought. Jesus so loved his children that he died for their sins. Gautama Buddha could have left this world in his evolved state of nirvana, but he came back to teach his Noble Truths. The Jews and Muslims also saw that doing good deeds for others was the basic ingredient to a truly productive and fulfilling life. Any social and political system that ignores compassion is rootless, according to my father."

"Yes, William, it makes me sad to admit that the Inner Party believes compassion is showing a basic human flaw, which is weakness. Totalitarian systems based on the accumulation of strength and control are doomed to fail. That's what my father believed. This is why I am going to assist you in your plan and why I want your father to lead us in a new world order. We must stop Big Bro before his plan for the eradication of the sick and elderly becomes even more a part of the insanity we now live. I loved the title of your father's last book, by the way. *The Insane Call Us Free*. The Inner Party is insane because it now believes life can be lived to the fullest only by eliminating the weakest and ugliest among us.

What's crazy about this thinking is that only the Young Socialists determine the criteria for what is weak and ugly. I happen to believe, for example, that black people and other colored people are not inherently ugly and lazy. And yet, Big Bro has circulated a dictum to that effect."

Both William and Judith stepped forward, their faces contorted in rage.

"What? So it *is* true! Big Bro is racist!" William shouted. He looked around for an MDP patrol to bust through the door and arrest him. All he could hear was the oceans' roar in the holographic action posters.

"Yes, I'm afraid it is. With this in mind, I must ask you both some questions about what you're willing to do for The Authority. The risk is obvious, but there are other dangers about which I want you to be fully aware. Are you willing to take the lives of Inner Party members?"

They both nodded.

"Are you willing to change your appearance and move to another campus anywhere around the world?"

Again, they gave their assent.

"If you find out anybody in your revolt is a traitor to our cause, and this includes me, are you willing to execute him or her on the spot?"

They looked at each other and then nodded.

"Finally, are you willing to abide by the philosophy of

family strength, healthy social values, and the democratic rule of law as outlined in Dr. Drury's New Constitution?"

"Yes," they both answered.

"All right then. I trust you both will be valiant members of The Authority. We will begin the plan as soon as William goes through the 40 Transference in the Ministry of Living Bliss. At the same moment you get your bliss implant, William, we will be activating step one in our plan." Jack Thornton drew a one in the air in front of him.

"The digital virus?" William asked.

"Yes, this was, quite ironically, the same method Big Bro was able to bring down the captain of industry and war back in 2028. We will now be implanting another virus especially made by your niece, William." Thornton smiled.

William remembered his dream. "Esther? How did you get her to create a virus? She's only seventeen years old!"

Judith touched William's arm. "She was recruited from college, William. Her skills at creating viruses are legend amongst the anonymous hackers online. I suppose you weren't aware of this also."

"No, I wasn't. It seems my family has a lot of secrets about which they failed to inform me. I hope I don't get any more surprises along the way." William began to walk toward the front door.

Jack Thornton and Judith Watimba followed him.

William shook both of their hands. "Don't we have a secret hand-shake or anything?"

"No time for such nonsense, William. Anything that calls attention to us is strictly forbidden," said Thornton. "Good luck in your 40 Transference. I'm certain you'll find it quite illuminating," he concluding, taking the security chip out the back of William's neck.

"Right. I guess I will," William said, and he walked out to the hover craft, where Thornton's house droid was waiting behind the controls.

Chapter Five

1. Upload virus into Ministries.

Esther knew nothing about The Authority and its overall plans. She was told by her mother, Ruth, that knowing this information would be too dangerous to her. All she knew was that she was to upload her virus into each of the ministries in San Diego. In addition, her virus would be transported to every campus in every city on the planet where others would be doing the same thing. All that Esther knew was that her virus would be shutting down the entire computer and remote-control Wi-Fi system of Big Bro, and this was good enough for her.

Like each member of her family, Esther hated Big Bro and all it stood for. She had heard the lectures of her grandfather, John, and the wisdom of her grandmother, Rose. Most of all, she was well informed as to the reality of the plan to destroy the sick and the elderly, and this made her furious. She hated her peers in school who had frequent casual sex, smoked Big Bro Weed, and basically followed the Party line without question. Although she dare not demonstrate an outward anger or opinion against them, she made it her mission in life to keep away from them as much as humanly possible.

However, as a nerd, she was privy to all the inner workings of the Big Bro technology and how it functioned, and she even had contacts who worked on station inside each of the ministries. They all played secretly developed computer games that made fun of Big Bro, and Esther was known as one of the best gamers on the Internet. She used the secret language of game messaging to find out where the best place was to upload a virus to infect the entire campus of Big Bro.

Esther was hunched over her tablet, typing out instructions to these secret connections inside the four ministries. Her frown of concentration emphasized the flashing motions of her fingers as she messaged. Her ruby lips were pursed, her black hair was wild and frizzy, and her leg tapped against the floor with her usual OCD energy. She wore the powder-blue overalls of a student in the College of Big Bro Communications and Technology, and she was occupied in the cafeteria. Hundreds of other students were also on their tablets or wearing their 3D visors, or even sexing-out in twos or threes to the music or virtual reality of some lame Erotica and Romance multimedia story. Most of them were also buzzing from the free hookahs that stood on the outer perimeters of the cafeteria like sentries of THC heaven. Esther never used marijuana, never sexed it with a brother or sister, and she had never seen one show on the E & R channel. She was completely devoted to her computer and to her immediate family.

Chasm into the deep drop.

Wait for the prime conductor to flame out.

Situate a righteous dinosaur in the Temple of Zeus.

Pull the plug.

Esther was instructing the four confederates who worked inside each of the ministries when to upload the virus. They all understood the code from their game-playing, and it would be a matter of minutes before each ministry in San Diego and throughout the cities of the world, at different times, would be infected by her virus or clones of her virus, and her job would be completed. She stopped typing and looked at the seconds on the clock of her tablet.

Ten…nine…eight…seven…six…five…four…three…two… one…infection!

Part 3

Chapter One

2. Stage riot to bring out the MDP.

Williamriode with Jack Thornton and his house droid, Baxter Bliss, over to the Ministry of Living Bliss for his 40 Transference ceremony. Every Outer and Inner Party member did this, so the ritual was well prepared and orderly. It consisted of the reading of some Mindfulvoice edict by Big Bro over the telescreen and the implant of the "bliss chip" into William by some Inner Party official. In this case, it was going to be his Minimind supervisor, Jack Thornton.

Mindfulvoice was the visual dictionary language that had replaced written and printed language. It was better, so said Big Bro, because it could be translated instantly into whichever specific language was needed for a particular geographical location. Also, there were no strict rules of grammar to cause consternation in the mind of Outer Party members. Finally, Mindfulvoice was much more real and in-the-moment communications. Laws became more emotive and brilliant, and the receiver of the law became a better receptor because there was no difficult burden of processing by the brain required as there was with the written word. In other words, there was much less ambiguity involved with Mindfulvoice.

William was thinking about the possibilities he was getting himself and his entire family into by cooperating with this plan. His steps felt leaden and without a sense of purpose. He was Othello, off the battlefield, walking into the tent of his enemies, knowing there was a trap waiting for him inside. All he wanted was to be with his family again, in one place, and if that had any chance of happening then he would do anything, including this. The cool air from the Inner Party air-conditioning hit his face as he stepped into the conference room.

There were about six Inner Party Members standing around the main table, and Jack pulled a polished wood chair out for William to sit down in. Three of the officials were male and three were female, and not one was over thirty. Their youthful, exuberant bodies were seated, and their radiant smiles instantly fixed upon his face. Their white denims almost shined back at him. Not one person of color was in the group. Jack Thornton turned down the lights, and the wall telescreen stopped broadcasting the news, and Big Bro came on.

"We are honored by this visit from one of our hard-working members in the Outer Party. I hereby transfer the biological name of Drury to you, Brother William. You will be joining your elders on the path to truth, wisdom and mental bliss, where every accommodation will be made to make the rest of your life in our society the most comfortable and intellectually challenging it can be. As you all know, every facet of the Young Socialists World Party exists to make the transference into the elder years the most enjoyable experience of your life. We in the Inner Party also make this transference, and it is the ultimate reward, giving us all complete equality at last. In the days before our grand revolutionary victory, the religionists had promised such comfort in their dogma, and yet it is we who have brought the reality into actual existence--in this world and not in a future one!"

"Yo Big Bro! Yo Big Bro!" the Inner Party Members around the table chanted.

Where were you when the grid was lost? William saw the lights in the room flicker once, twice, and then he watched as they went out along with Big Bro's face, and they were left in total darkness. William could hear the chairs being moved, and then he felt the force of a hand on his back.

"Let's go! It's time to move out," the voice said, and William supposed it was Jack Thornton. It was time for the riot.

The voices of the Inner Party members were calm, under the circumstances. William heard one of the women say, "The emergency generators should kick-in shortly," and she was correct. As Thornton and William were moving into the stairway shaft, the lights returned, and the building began to hum again.

"Will this affect our plan?" William said.

"No, if the virus worked, then the ministries will not be functioning. The Wi-Fi remote controls will not work. The droids will be frozen in place all over San Diego as will the drones. The spy cameras will not work, and telescreens will be down. Only the emergency lights will go on by back-up local generator power. We will only have to contend with the MDP because they are powered differently for emergencies like these. We believe there are no more than five hundred of these special force droids, but we had to estimate a certain number of our own who will be terminated during the riot." Thornton pushed through the emergency door at the bottom of the stairs, and it opened with some effort.

"Terminated? You mean, you were planning to sacrifice our members?"

"Yes, William Drury. Your father knew this was going to be necessary also. It's part of any revolt. Sacrifices must be made to ensure the goal of The Authority is accomplished. We must lead the special group over to the Ministry of Freedom to get weapons. Your special cell phone encryption software is working perfectly. I am able to text them without any fear of Inner Party technologists tapping into our messages." Thornton was busy punching into his phone's keypad as they sprinted down the street toward the Ministry of Freedom on Sixth Avenue downtown.

The riot was happening out in Balboa Park. William could see a crowd of about three hundred Outer Party members attempting to push over the enormous statue of Big Bro in the center of the park near the Museums to the Revolution of 2028. As they strained together, they dug in their heels, pushed their shoulders to the cement base of the statue, and groaned in tandem. They sang out in unison, "Fuck Big Bro! Fuck Big Bro! Fuck Big Bro!"

Despite the violence, William felt a powerful resurgence of pride in his fellow brothers and sisters when the MDP squadron appeared. The tall bots marched toward the park over the bridge off Sixth Avenue, their jackboots gleaming in the sunshine, their heels thudding on the pavement, and their laser bio-demobilizing rifles held high above their two-faced, helmeted heads. These Mindful Droid Protectors were the last line of defense for the Inner Party, and they were ferocious in their programmed killing skills.

The Big Bro statue was teetering precariously as the MDP troopers came upon the crowd, and when the effigy began to fall, a great cheer rose into the afternoon air, making life seem alive once again after the many years of remotely controlled dictatorship. The rifles came down from over the robots' heads, and the MDP beaded their scopes onto the heads of the rioters.

This is not at night, Father. This is not happening at night! This is happening right now! William held his breath as he ran down Sixth Avenue with Thornton. His eyes, however, were focused on the carnage happening next to El Cid's statue in the park. The crumbled form of Big Bro was soon intermingled with the fallen, headless bodies of their comrades, as the lasers exploded their craniums like ruby-red grapefruit that burst apart like miniature red dwarf suns.

3. Confiscate weapons from the Ministry of Freedom.

While the other revolutionaries were being slaughtered out in the park, there were about fifty more who were waiting for William and Jack at the Ministry of Freedom. The distraction had worked, as there were no MDP to greet them as Thornton quickly passed out security chips to authorize all of them for entry into the building. William knew this was where Big Bro's office was located, and the darkness required the night goggles that were on the faces of the droid guards standing in front of the ministry. These were remotely-controlled droids, so the virus had stopped them in their tracks. All the remote-controlled droids and drones were run by Wi-Fi, so they were down with the virus.

They looked like black statues of robot soldiers greeting them, as William snatched a pair of goggles from one of them and strapped the infrared spectacles around his head. He pushed open the front door and entered closely behind another brother. They all followed Jack Thornton in a mad dash downstairs to the basement of the building where the armory was located. When the door to the armory was opened, William could hear a high-pitched whine that seemed strange. After fourteen of The Authority had entered the armory, there was a flash of light from above, and down from the ceiling came a storm of arrows. To his right and to his left, William could see his comrades being struck in their heads with these shafts of razor-sharp titanium-tipped weapons from centuries past.

"They must have put them in recently!" Jack Thornton shouted, ducking down, as an arrow shot over his head in a near miss. "They are battery-powered, no doubt," he added.

William leaped over a fallen body and smashed into a pile of stacked laser rifles. He picked one up and aimed it at a spot where he thought the arrows were coming from. It was a surreal vision to see these green streaks of death piercing the darkness all around the room and to hear the expiry screams of his fallen brothers and sisters. If they didn't put this arrow cannon out of commission soon, there would be nobody left to use the rifles.

"How do I shoot this damned thing?" William shouted.

"Pull the lever down on the bottom of the stock to arm the laser, and then squeeze on the padded treadle below the scope," Jack instructed him.

William aimed up toward the corner of the room's ceiling where the arrows were coming from, and he pulled the lever. The rifle's barrel lit-up with a red glowing pulsation. He found the soft trigger mechanism below the end of the scope and squeezed slowly.

A burst of laser light erupted from the rifle and shot toward the ceiling, which was about fifty feet above him. He missed, but William could see a large circular metal box when the light struck the wall nearby. He quickly shot the rifle again, and this time it struck home. The box exploded, but there was another surprise hidden within this booby-trap. A thick cloud of smoke came wafting down toward them.

"Don't breathe! It's a poison gas!" Thornton yelled. "Grab a rifle and get the hell out of here!"

Each of the invaders grabbed a rifle and followed William out of the room. When they were all standing together outside the Ministry of Freedom, The Authority had fifty armed troopers ready to lead the way into the Inner Party offices in each of the four ministries. Dozens more revolutionaries, wearing gas masks, were rushing into the building and heading down the stairs to the armory. Hopefully, they would ultimately be armed well enough to capture Big Bro himself when it was all over.

Chapter Two

4. Invade the Inner Party offices and return control to The Authority.

No date. About six days after my 40 Transference.

I am writing in my journal right now. I don't have to hide what I'm doing from Big Bro because he was captured. My reward for being part of the revolt was to be allowed to follow in my father's footsteps and write whatever and whenever I wish to write. In fact, since my father is now the leader in the San Diego Campus, I can even get my work published in a printed book, if I so *choose. Jack Thornton says the museum to the 2028 Revolution is being completely upgraded, and he wants my father's books, as well as my diary, to be featured documents within it. I still can't believe all of this is true.*

I never went with the other armed members to the ministries. The violence was making me ill, and I told Jack Thornton he would not do well with me retching all over my laser gun. Besides, I would probably get somebody else killed because of my intense fear. He kindly told me I would not be needed during the raids into the Inner Party offices and that I was quite a hero anyway, as my actions had allowed the looting of the armory inside the Ministry of Freedom.

My father would be chastising me right now if he weren't at the Ministry of Mindfulness broadcasting his weekly "Message to The Authority." He would be telling me that my writing was too much "telling" and not enough "showing." I would argue that I am not writing fiction or even creative non-fiction. I am writing a personal diary, which, as the online dictionary tells me is "a daily record, usually private, especially of the writer's own experiences, observations, feelings, attitudes, etc." It is such a relief to believe one's own thoughts can be respected enough to be read and understood by important members of the society in which you risked your life to put into power. This is reward enough to me.

I can tell you one thing. If I had been there on the day the Inner Party offices were invaded, and Big Bro was captured, I would have tried to stop what was happening.

You see, despite the silent holocaust of Big Bro's plan to eliminate the old and enfeebled, it was not a violent process. What Jack Thornton's group did when they punished the Inner Party members who were part of Big Bro's cadre of planners was not acceptable to me. They cut out their tongues. Oh yes, and Jack has insisted that these pieces of the human anatomy be preserved and put on display inside the museum in Balboa Park. He also reported that there were even more abhorrent atrocities that had been committed during raids into other Big Bro campuses around the world. What we did was actually not very inhumane, compared to what had happened elsewhere. Thornton explained that the tongues were severed from the mouths of Inner Party members— especially Big Bro—as punishment for lying to the people. "Now that your father is our leader, the people will be listening to the truth," Thornton explained. "We are building our new social reality from the ground up, beginning with the word Dr. Drury said was the term which makes humans more humane."

I don't know exactly what Jack Thornton means by this, but I imagine our move to his place in the La Jolla Hills has a lot to do with it. My entire family is now residing here, including my mother, Rose, with her increasingly debilitating Lewy Body Dementia. What makes this much different from her life in the Gerontology Units is the fact that we humans do all the caring for her—not the droids. In addition, as a reward for our role in the successful overthrow of Big Bro, we no longer have to work inside the ministries. We can do all our work at home, as a family, and this was the best part of our revolution.

As I stated earlier, my father is downtown recording his weekly message to the masses. My sister is in the bedroom taking care of my mother. It has relieved my father quite a bit to have our family taking care of her. If truth be told, I believe it was my father's hatred for the population of droids taking care of her that probably led to his becoming such a key part of The Authority's revolt. His father, my grandfather, Gerald Drury, was one of the first revolutionaries against the droid occupation, if you want to call it that. His farm in Illinois, where my relatives come from, was one of the first farms chosen for upgrading to droid services, and my father's memories of that time are recorded in this diary.

Jack Thornton ensures me that the economy will no longer be controlled remotely by such technologies. In fact, we have been authorized to switch places with the Inner Party, as they are doing the work inside the ministries now—all of them—and we are allowed to live in these exclusive homes. We are encouraged to grow our own gardens with vegetables and even raise small numbers of livestock like chickens, pigs and cows. It's quite a sight to see all these fancy homes with the chickens in the yards and the children playing all over the neighborhoods.

Later that same afternoon, no date.

My father has returned from his speaking engagement over the network's digital airwaves, and he seems quite exuberant. He has always told me he gets high from his lectures, and I believe him. This honor of being chosen to be the symbolic leader of The Authority makes us all so proud. He has told us that there will be many people of color in the Inner Party. However, since there will no longer be any designations of "inner" or "outer," we will all be part of the new government's structure. He says peace will still be the will of the people, but no longer will the drones and droids be for the service and protection of the exclusives in the Inner Party. They will be used to protect the freedoms of everyone. There will also be no public displays of sex or drug use, although private use will be permitted.

It is difficult to believe at this point, but my father has told me there will be no need for weapons of any kind in the near future. He has been informed by Jack Thornton that The Authority is taking his idea about creating a society wherein the highest standard of humanity will be taught and acted out in daily life. Compassion, according to my father, will be the watch-word for all laws created under The Authority. We will also be returning to the freedoms of religion and cultural identity that were missing for so long in our world. Father says that as long as we create the atmosphere for compassion, there will be no weapons needed, and religions will be able to thrive at last by exhibiting their common core beliefs that always returned to the noble idea of the Golden Rule: Treat others as you want to be treated.

I am so very sad to inform you, but my mother, Rose, has passed away. One moment we were listening to her tell us her latest hallucination, and the next moment she was staring into space, and her breathing stopped. Due to the stiffness of her limbs caused by the disease, her hands were held across her chest in the bed, and I kept thinking about those Pharaohs in Egypt who believed they could carry objects with them into the next life. That's why I put some new roses under those arms, and we all just stood there crying together as a family at last.

When she began speaking about what she was experiencing in her vision, I was quite shocked. Rose did not recognize any of us, and she told us she was standing alone inside the bottom tomb beneath one of the giant pyramids in Egypt. She could feel death inside her, she said, but she could also feel the priests' cold hands upon her body, as they implanted the embalming fluids inside her. They told her she was going to live forever and that there would be no more suffering where she was going. She was elated, and the smile on her face made all of us smile. We had grown quite accustomed to our mother's hallucinations, as the doctor informed us that with Lewy Body Dementia a great amount of endorphins are accumulated in the brain cells, which causes the visionary states of paranoia to become quite frequent toward the end of life.

Jack Thornton came into the bedroom just before Rose expired, and she pointed her shaking hand toward him, her face grimacing in pain. "He would have you believe in eternal life! He is the Pharaoh and the blasphemer! Kill him! Kill him!" she said, and then she passed on.

"I thought you told me your wife was a Baptist," Jack Thornton told my father, chuckling, perhaps unsure of *what he should say. With all that had to be done downtown, Thornton did not have time to see what exactly our mother had become. He just thought she was demented, and these delusions were not familiar to him.*

"My wife was a woman of the world, Mr. Thornton. We need to respect her wishes to be buried in a Christian cemetery, however."

Thornton turned to us, and his head moved to concentrate deeply on each of our faces, one by one, as the room had become quiet and funereal on its own. Such moments as these are standard in the life of any family in mourning. What he said to us are words I hastened to write down here for the record.

"I want to show you all what we have planned for your mother and for you. As the Golden Family of The Authority, we want you to have a most revered place in the collective memories of our new world of peace and tranquility. Come out with me now to the museum, and I'll explain what we'll be doing."

Still later that same afternoon. No date.

We followed Jack Thornton into the museum. It still had the architecture from the 1915-1916 Panama-California Exhibition that according to Jack's father commemorated the opening of the Panama Canal to the shipping trade. Of course, nothing was taller than one story, but Thornton assured us the new government would be restoring the museums back to their tall and statuesque glory days. For example, there used to be a two-hundred foot tower next to the museum he was taking us into, which had a round, domed roof with blue tiles inlaid into it. Thornton said his father told him it was an ironic statement being made at the turn of the Twentieth Century, in that the building looked like the entrance to a church, with statues of Catholic Mission leader Father Junìpero Serra and Conquistador Vasco Nuñez de Balboa inlaid on the front, but it was actually a monument to the waning power of the Church. It was a museum to prove the scientific certainty of Evolution. The exhibits testified to the fact that all of nature was a product of natural selection and evolutionary forces and not any kind of divine intervention or Adam and Eve fairytale.

Of course, Big Bro had converted this museum into a monument to the Revolution of 2028, but now Jack Thornton explained that it would become a living monument to The Authority of Compassion, and we were going to be a major exhibition inside. However, when we entered the main exhibit room, what we saw caused my father to grab his chest, and my sister Ruth screamed. It was a simulated classroom setting, and in front of the old-fashioned blackboard was my mother, Rose! She was no longer the frail, dying woman we had just seen. Instead, this was the vibrant, forty-something professor from our youth. Her black hair had only a few streaks of gray, and her face was as beautiful as we remembered it. Her eyelashes were long, the dimples stood out in her ebony cheeks, and those thick, passionate eyebrows arched above her animated brown eyes and full, pink lips. Those were the same warm lips my father had first *written about and then had given those writings to me to put inside my first entry into this diary.*

"She looks so real!" said Ruth, finally composing herself.

"Watch," said Thornton.

We did watch, in complete horror and fascination, as our mother came to life in front of us. She began to pace, as she was, like our father, a moving dynamo when she spoke. Her African dress was a long white Dashiki with embroidered grape vines on the sleeves, and I remembered the white uniforms of the Inner Party Members during my aborted 40 Transference ceremony.

"Welcome, my family, to the exhibition commemorating teaching as it was conducted many years ago. I have been chosen to give this brief lecture on what compassionate authority means to us. I understand that lectures are not the way to teach in this modern era of WiFi and global Internet communications, but the establishing principle of our society is the family. We are going to keep the family unit intact, and all work, recreation and communications will flow from those units. No longer will we isolate our people in the name of freedom, whether it's sexuality, consumerism or recreational drug use. The family teaches that compassionate authority gives all of us an opportunity to grow and to be nurtured to achieve our highest goals and abilities. When you know you will always be welcomed, you will recognize that the family unit is being coordinated with love at the center. My husband, John, saw me as the love of his life, and we both tried to extend

that love to our children. We hope all of you in the new family of The Authority can achieve your own inner peace and harmonious love to build relationships with the wider branches in the Family of Humanity. God bless us all!"

The image of our mother lecturing inside a classroom was too much for my father. He began to weep, and soon we were all crying. She looked so life-like. It was as if the wonders of scientific robotics had returned our mother to us as quickly as she had passed from this world.

My mother's father, Samuel Wilton, had been a preacher in Memphis, Tennessee, and when she went to college it almost killed him. His wife had died early on in their marriage, so Rose was his only connection with the feminine joy he had experienced with his wife. He turned against my mother when the Revolt of 2028 began, as he thought the revolution was inspired by the Devil, and when he heard my mother was working as a teacher in the college of Big Bro, he visited her classroom and began to picket outside. He held a giant cross, yelled damning scripture quotations wearing his black pastoral suit, and that's when the Mindful Droid Protectors came out to the campus and arrested him. Before they took him away, one of them reached inside her father's jacket, pulled out a copy of the Bible, and put the black book inside the grinder blades that were inside his metal mouth. She never saw her father after that day, and we assumed he had been vaporized. Religions had been banned by Big Bro, and her father was a useless commodity.

We were now very proud that our mother, and my father's wife, would be memorialized in this museum exhibit. We each went up to her and felt her face, hands and hair. They seemed very real to the touch.

"How did you do this?" my father asked Jack Thornton.

"We have now developed our animatronics so that we can use the DNA genome of any human and form any human into a programmed android. We copy the genetic structure of the person, in this case your mother, and we duplicate it into digital format. Then, we replicate the person using our 3D pattern duplicator. Each and every cell is perfectly copied and duplicated so that you see what we have here."

"But how did you get her voice and her way of acting so perfect?" Ruth asked.

"Again, the brain itself is nothing more than an organ, and it can also be copied. We simply digitized the uniquely configured brain cells and all the organs of speech. The organs used, of course, include the lips, teeth, tongue, alveolar ridge, hard palate, soft palate, uvula and glottis." As Thornton listed the organs of speech, he put his right hand up to mother's mouth, opened it wide, and pointed with his other hand's index finger to each item on his list. When he came to her tongue, I couldn't help but shudder involuntarily at the thought of what he had done to Big Bro and the other Inner Party Members.

Despite these obvious technological advancements, I still had a fear in the hidden recesses of my being about what was happening. If Thornton could perform such heinous acts against his adversaries, how difficult can it be to become his enemy? I enjoyed my mother's speech, but that animatronic device was not my mother, no matter how exacting the DNA copy had been. Cells and organs were constantly changing in the human body, so a copy was merely a freeze-frame photograph of one split-second in time. My mother would not grow old, change her habits, become a spontaneous being or even contract Lewy Body Dementia. She would remain in what Big Bro would have called the "Eternal Now," never behaving like a human again.

We thought the museum was a fine idea, as our populace could visit to see what was written by my father to establish The Authority, and then watch my mother give her lecture. Jack Thornton told us that our DNA would also be used to create other exhibits.

"We're creating a new way to run the world, and we want all who visit to see how it began," said Thornton. "We'll have museums like this in every city and village around the world," he added.

"You mean, the local revolutionaries will be featured, right? Certainly you don't mean our family," I said.

"That's right, William. The local members will be featured, but each revolution happened because of your efforts, however, so there will be one exhibit to show your family and especially your father's writings. Your niece,

Esther, will also be featured, since her virus was the way we brought down Big Bro around the world." Thornton was standing next to Esther, and he patted her purple-streaked black hair with his big hand.

"That's not inspiring," said Esther, tilting her head away from his hand.

"Esther!" said Ruth. "Don't you want to be a motivation to other young members of our authority?"

"My work requires anonymity. How do you think I was able to do this in the first place?" Esther said.

"She's right. We won't have an Esther exhibition," said Thornton. "I'm glad you pointed that out."

5. *Return the power to the people and to their families.*

When we returned to La Jolla Hills and Thornton's home, the last phase of the plan was set to be put into action. I thought it was amazing how quickly the elements had come together, and how successfully every aspect worked, but Thornton's explanation of using Big Bro's technology against him was a good one. Even in the days before the 2028 Revolution, society had been moving more into using technology to make human activities more convenient and interconnected, but the obvious backlash was what ultimately resulted. If all members weren't in accord with the system, then the system could be fairly easily overturned and taken over.

Thornton wanted to explain to all of us how the family units were going to be the hubs of all compassionate *work throughout The Authority. We sat around his living room, in the variety of orange chairs and inflated glow cushions. Father preferred to stand, as his arthritis was acting up on him. Thornton stood in the center of our family wheel and addressed us. I jotted down everything longhand, when I could, in my diary. I enjoyed using the old technology of handwriting, as it connected me with the past that my parents said was so very valuable to progress in human society. Since Thornton's father had been a history professor, he also understood this value, and I was encouraged to keep a record. For these longer speeches, I did use the recording function on my phone, but I later transcribed them into my diary by hand.*

"I want your family to be the first to understand how our workflow will be progressing using the template we have been developing, in secret, for many years. As you may know, I was beginning my own technological development of resources, you saw an example at the museum today, and when the underground revolution contacted me, the tools we needed to use were already developed. We plan to use these tools as the method of delivering our family-centered social structure to the world's population. First of all, all decisions will be made as a family unit, so each family living in our appointed homes will be monitored and placed online to be able to send out their family vote in a micro-second, if needed. We have divided each geographic area into what we call Family Compassion Centers. There will be a total of nearly three billion of these centers, around the world, and each one will act as a hub of decision-making for a variety of purposes. Of course, not all of our community

will be inside these special homes, the way you are, since the world population is now 9.6 billion. Some of the city workers will be residing in smaller, yet still comfortable surroundings in the cities, towns and villages around the world. They will also be allowed to vote, however, and this is at the heart of our system of compassionate family values."

"What kinds of decisions will be made?" my father asked.

"Good question, Dr. Drury. Way back at the early turn of the Twenty-First Century, technologists and political scientists were thinking about how to make a democracy work using what then was the primitive Internet. The idea about one person and one direct vote was dropped, mostly because of the greedy lobbyists and politicians, who wanted to make a business out of democracy and electing people who were supposed to represent their best interests. When this failed to work, as we know, the revolution happened, and Big Bro's system of governance came into being. We, on the other hand, plan to use the system of monitoring each citizen, which was in place, and turn it into a democracy for the best interests of the people. Any person in our world family, aged sixteen and over, will have a vote on the variety of proposals that will be put to them to read online, and each family can even print copies to be discussed and argued about right in the home. Each person in the family unit will then be able to cast his or her vote over the interconnected digital hubs, where all family votes will be tallied, and the results will be posted for all to

read on their phones or other digital devices."

My father frowned. "That's all well and good. I'm certain you have the technology to do this, but who will draft these proposals that need to be voted on in order pass with a majority?"

"Yes, and what kind of voting security will be in place?" Ruth asked.

"Any family unit or individual in any family home can draft a proposal to be put up for a vote by the majority. A screening committee will sift out any of the completely illogical or dangerous proposals and reject them out of hand. The proposals that are approved will go on to be placed up on our websites to be voted upon. As for security, we are not leaving that up to the chance of the digital web. Instead, in the next few weeks, we will perform minor surgery on each voting member to implant a voting chip that will receive signals from the brain when powered on. Each of these chips will have a unique coding that cannot be duplicated, so when they send in their votes, they will also have this unique code encrypted inside the signal being sent. The Family Compassion Centers will make certain each vote has this unique code by matching the code against our master list, and only then will the vote be registered as authentic."

"I like it," I said. "So the people can propose anything they believe will show some kind of compassionate purpose, is that the rule?"

"Quite right, William. After all, isn't this the purpose of

human existence? This lack of compassionate thinking has been the fly in the ointment of democratic movements throughout history. Socialistic enterprises, like Big Bro and Communism, failed because the individual was seen as merely a tool for the Inner Party and its selfish purposes. My father said, for example, that in what was called China, the Communist Party hi-jacked the Capitalistic movement in the early Twenty-First Century, and most of the people ending up working for a system that put them into Enterprise Zones but failed to give them living wages or to protect them against the increasing spread of pollution in the air. The entire planet suffered from that little experiment."

"I can see the logic you have," said Ruth. "If we teach everyone to think with the best interests of the family in their minds, the proposals will not be filled with the element of greed that seems to be the ingredient in the past which proved to be our downfall."

"I'm so happy you all see it my way. You'll see society change so much for the better. New technical genius will sprout forth with these family-centered proposals, and we will gradually become a true democracy of one person, one vote, and not the antiquated version of representational votes that led to so much corruption and bribery." Thornton walked toward the door. He was going back to the city to complete the technical details for our new reality.

Three years later, no date.

Although I was enthused by his optimistic lecture,

something inside me again wriggled to the surface to claim a place in my brain. It kept working at my thoughts until the example of what else his system could produce came to me in the form of the back story concerning a private business that a physics professor got involved in out of New York City and at his private retreat in New Mexico.

Families, it seemed, were not all the perfect golden kind that we seemed to be. After I finished reading his story, I became even more worried about what was really happening in this brave new business world of The Authority. It was as if this one example were a blood moon rising to shine its light of a doomed future on all of us. I began to collect the stories from other new enterprises around the world of The Authority. I will now reproduce these stories for you, one by one, and you will certainly see how this new brand of family values was being demonstrated. There was something going on that was like a cancerous tumor you first spot on your body as a small mole, and then you have to investigate deeper and spread your search in wider concentric circles to take in the complete horrific vision of how it has spread.

Chapter Three

Report from the Professor. No date.

At first, I had this immediate feeling that my body was imploding. As a particle physicist, I am aware of the entropic characteristics that all matter possesses. It is the reality that all atheists like me has to face. No matter how assiduously we work to create a sensually provocative habitat, time will take its toll on our physical appearance and, indeed, on our ability to appreciate life itself. Thank goodness, we also have ways of sparking energy into our bodies in order to combat the inevitable fact of entropy. As a sixty-eight-year-old male college professor, I was not going to fall victim to entropy and its all-consuming death. Instead, as my wife, who is a psychotherapist for persons suffering from eating disorders likes to say, "You have to feed the fire to stay human."

We have a lovely vacation villa in New Mexico called "La Casa de Mañana." My wife, Geraldine, and I like to use it in the winter, when the snows hit upper Manhattan. Geraldine appreciates the fact that we are not getting any younger, and that gravity has taken hold on her body as well. Therefore, she knows about my little hobby, and, in fact, she was very supportive when I brought the idea to her to discuss over wine and Gouda, just before we left for New Mexico.

Geraldine is a tall woman, and she wears her clothes stylishly. She has kept her figure, and she is proud to be an excellent example to her patients, who are quite the opposite, in many cases, having succumbed to the American "junk food monster," as Geri likes to call it. Geri and I met in college; she was in grad school at NYU, as was I, and we hit it off almost immediately. We were both Libertarians, politically, and we were enamored of the works of Ayn Rand and Ron Paul. Most of all, we understood the purpose for existence: to maximize pleasure and to minimize pain. Indeed, the most advanced societies in the world understood this, and their daily activities reflected the credo of hedonism that we subscribed to.

Many of our friends and relatives often ask us about how we stay so optimistically young in our attitudes and in our activities. The answer is at the heart of Libertarian values. We place our own happiness before any that the political or governmental construct can fashion. Therefore, when I explained how my hobby could be expanded into a more developed enterprise on the new Internet of The Authority, Geri was quite enthusiastic. After all, she also would often "recharge her batteries," as she liked to call it. We were constantly looking for new ways to enhance our enjoyment of sensual pleasures, and my idea was certainly doing that.

"You remember how difficult it was to find an escort service in New Mexico?" I asked Geri, toking on our large, Egyptian water pipe. I have a card for medicinal marijuana from The Authority because of my back pain. I like to refresh my supply of THC with the cool Aquafina that I keep inside the hookah. The psychoactive hallucinogen also assists me in making creative leaps of insight when I'm planning a computer project. My mind is very linear when I don't smoke marijuana. The drug, as it has always done, allows me to make new connections in non-linear ways.

"Yes, you were quite perturbed by all the calling you had to do," Geri said, placing her index finger on my nose and smiling at me. Her captivatingly aquamarine eyes glistened in the candlelight like beacons of future passion.

"I think I've found a solution to all the problems we've had procuring a suitable escort. I've kept the email addresses of the business people we've hired and enjoyed in the past, and I recently approached them with my idea. They are all quite agreeable, and we have thus determined to open our new service in beta form beginning next week."

"Service? You're not going to rent that gorgeous body of yours, are you?" Geri giggled.

"Of course not! I am simply going to use the software program I use at school in order to organize and establish a structured and profitable escort service." I dragged on the pipe and blew smoke rings. I always picture myself as the caterpillar sitting on the giant psychedelic mushroom in *Alice in Wonderland*. Whoooo are yoooooo?

"How will it work? It sounds very interesting, but the devil is always in the details, as you like to point out to me," said Geri.

"First off, the interface will be plain and peaceful. One banner image will show the tranquil desert and shadowy mountains of New Mexico. There will be referrals from the girls who get prospective clients off their own web sites, and we will also get prospects that create an account on the main web site I will create. There will be three levels of participation. The first level will place the client on probation. This allows the client access to one escort for one appointment. This is where my genius comes into play."

"Oh, I knew there would be some of that," Geri said.

"The girl will email me with the details of the first appointment. What did the client ask for? How much did he or she pay? How did he or she behave? If the client performs admirably, then he or she can move into the next category of participation, which is verified status. This will reassure my customers, the providers of the escort services, that these verified clients have passed the most important hurdle. Then, after the client has successfully participated in five such rendezvous, he or she will be moved up into the top category on my organizational structure, sponsorship. Sponsorship will allow a client to choose amongst the variety of available escorts, and it will also permit them to rate each escort. These ratings will be made available to sponsors only. In addition, I will also visit these top-rated escorts in order to provide a quality check on their services. This last gambit will also give me a boost of energy to make our love life that much more satisfactory, my darling."

I moved toward Geri, and she opened her arms to me. We kissed passionately, and our bodies soon became one. "Howard!" she cried, in our usual pantomime of our favorite literary characters from our favorite novel, *The Fountainhead*, by Ayn Rand. "Dominique!" I answered, pulling her on top of my rising skyscraper.

My new hobby was quite successful until I began receiving emails from someone who called him or herself "lonewolf13." I knew this individual was going to be trouble when the salutation in the email began, "Dear

Needle-dick the Bug Fucker," and continued with a rash of argumentative vindictiveness that challenged not only my manhood but also the core of my philosophical being. It was if this person were spawned from the depths of Big Bro-era Socialism and had become my adversarial doppelgänger. Not only did he or she mock my Libertarian principles, but the fabric of my very being was also being refuted:

what gives u the right to judge how somebuddy fucks, u dum kunt? u fucking ad for erecktail disfuction! the people should choose on there own. they dont need no fony professer to judge for them.

As I learned later, this was but a warning shot across the bow of my ship. Despite the obviously illiterate emails, this person was a true hacker and spy with computer skills which far surpassed my own.

The real war began between us following an online debate that started on the discussion board created for sponsor-level participants. Lonewolf13 must have hacked into the board and read the debate, because he or she knew exactly what was said and who said it.

The argument began over legalization of drugs and prostitution. We were all in basic agreement that by making victimless crimes like these legal, society could reap the benefits in terms of lower disease rates, fewer crimes by addicts, and raising the level of clientele quality.

That's when the hacker piped up. He told us we were full

of excrement and that it was a modern fact that creativity in video games, music and in movies did more than any drug in the world could do for one's imagination, and that sexually transmitted diseases have developed a resistance to known treatments, and no birth control was 100% effective. Also, profit should remain in the hands of the independent business entrepreneur.

i thot thats what u were all into u libertines! Free enterprise and all that shit.

I told this person if he were so smart, then he should show us what he meant by using specific examples. He said he would and that I should meet him at an undisclosed location. He was going to send me an encrypted email with the address, and I should meet him there the next day.

The encrypted address he gave me was 1526 South Adobe Falls Road in Santa Fe, which turned out to be an abandoned warehouse. It looked like a rat-infested hovel out of an old Big Bro novel, and I was expecting some horrendous display of foreign refugees from Big Bro, shivering in a dark room, huddled under the watchful eye of Inner Party pimps.

Instead, the most beautiful woman I have ever seen padded her barefoot way into the dark room, a brilliant light from the ceiling following her every step. She wore a flowing white tunic, obviously Grecian, and her blonde hair was crowned with a halo of golden roses; she had a long sash around her waist made of spun gold. With each step, her alabaster legs were unveiled, and my eyes followed these legs up her body, to her roundly firm breasts, and they finally stopped at her face. There was also a misty glow that smelled of jasmine and roses, and I could hear the sound of water gurgling over rocks.

The stimulation from gazing at her body became immediately irrelevant when I looked into her face. This was the only woman I have ever seen whose face gave me an erection. Her eyes were ocean blue, and her nose was aquiline above pouty, swollen pink lips. The dimples on either side of her mouth caused a firestorm of desire inside me that made me want to leap at her from the shadows like an aroused leopard.

"I am so glad you could visit us, Dr. Spence. We have so much to see and discuss and not much time to do it in," the gorgeous creature said, clasping my hands. Her flesh was warm, and I felt like I could walk with her forever as she led me down the corridor to a locked room. However, I was surprised that this woman had met me and not lonewolf13, and I told her as much.

"Oh, Sebastian is our computer technician. He is constantly prowling about looking for mischief. You must not judge a book by its cover. Sebastian may seem a bit crude, but his heart is in the right place. He is entirely with us and with our overall philosophy," she smiled, and those dimples cast a spell over me. It was as difficult to argue with her as it would be to argue with a movie star.

As the door opened, an intercom voice came on to explain what I was seeing. What I was actually seeing was a room filled with hundreds of devices suspended from the ceiling, attached to the walls and coming up from the floor. There were fountains, dildos, leather pants and vests, whips, chains, flowers, perfumes, mirrors, vibrators, and lotions. The voice-over was clear, precise and informational. It was as if I were touring an exhibit in some museum or art compilation.

Aphrodite's Pleasure Palace gives the client choice. As the foundation of any democratic system, we want our customers to have their sexual fantasy needs met no matter how extravagant or seemingly perverse they might appear to the society at large. Aristotle believed that entertainment must provide catharsis; that is, the best way to prevent rape, violence and sexual aberrations in the social arena, is to allow the public to experience these events artistically, in our rooms.

What happened next was so shocking to my system that I still find it difficult putting the words down. Another woman, almost as beautiful as my hostess, came into the room from a side door, followed by a big beefy man dressed in black, his head covered by a hood. At first, he ordered the woman to undress, and she complied, dropping her kimono to the floor to reveal a shapely form, with firm, uplifted breasts and a black patch of pubis. The man walked over to her and began slapping her—first in the face, gently, and then on her thighs and buttocks. Her white skin began to take on a reddish hue, and her breathing came in quick gasps. As he began to strike her more violently, her nipples became engorged and she let out squeals of pain. But then, the big ape picked one of the large bull whips off the wall and began thrashing her repeatedly about the shoulders, breasts, legs and ass. Large, bloody welts formed, and she finally fell to the floor.

"Make him stop!" I shouted, becoming enraged.

However, he did not stop. In fact, he strapped on a gigantic dildo and walked over to her supine body until he stood directly above her head. I'll never forget the look of ultimate terror on her face as this beast pushed that 20-inch tumescent flange into her mouth and crushed it into the back of her skull. She gagged, she writhed on the floor like a snake, and when she finally succumbed, her bladder and bowels released, sending a putrid odor wafting all around the room.

That's when I passed out, I guess, and was awakened inside a room that contained a giant water fountain, classical music that streamed throughout, and my hostess was standing over me with that same giant dildo strapped to her waist.

I screamed bloody murder, of course, but she just laughed and unfastened the dildo so that it fell to the floor with a plop.

"What in the hell just happened in there?" I asked, rising up on my elbows in the turquoise chase lounge to stare into those blue eyes.

"Wasn't it realistic?" she asked. "She was an example of our latest model, the Z50-TX. Many of our members choose that model because they have life-like internal organs, a respiratory system, as well as the demonstrated evacuation and blood stream flow."

"Are you telling me that woman was not real?" I asked.

"Of course not! This was what we brought you over to see. We supply the latest robot technology available. Unless our clients can experience every fantasy they may have, our purposes will not be fulfilled. With every Z50-TX that is used, one real woman out there on the streets of the world will be saved. That's the way we look at it. Our clients believe they are getting real women, yet, as you have seen, we supply them with our robotic women who appear to be tortured, but they are simply performing their programmed activities."

As she said this, the same woman from the torture room walked into our grotto. She was smiling, and there were no physical marks, bruises or scratches anywhere to be seen on her lusciously naked form.

"Where are you people located? I have done research into sex robots for my own purposes, and I have found no such realistic device out there. The most they had was a robotic rubber version not much better than the inflatable Blowjob Bettys that are found in your neighborhood sex shop. I'm not saying I agree with your ideas about purging emotions and all that Greek hoopla, but you really do have a convincing product! Where can I get one?"

"I am glad you asked, Dr. Spence. We have been monitoring your little enterprise, and we would like to extend an offer to you. We need some sales reps out there in the public who can best represent our interests. Because we only supply our services after a thorough screening and personal invitation, we need to have professionals we can trust exhibiting what we have to offer. We believe you could be one such professional."

"Listen. I was just thinking about my personal enjoyment. What do I have to do to get one of these ladies in my own house?"

"Of course, you can avail yourself of her beauty, whenever you wish, but we need to introduce our services to a wider and more sophisticated audience and clientele. Can you help us?" She smiled, and those dimples won me over.

What Aphrodite wanted was for me to introduce Jasmine (the name I gave her) to my colleagues in the academic world. I supposed she was charging quite a bit of money to partake in these sexual antics, and I was hoping that if I could be a good sales rep, perhaps she would include me in the profit she was undoubtedly making.

As Geri and I played with our new toy in bed, we examined her body from head to foot. Not only was she perfectly developed, with life-like skin, motion and breathing, she was also a wonderful conversationalist. We tried out our entire repartee on her: science, humanities, current events and popular culture. She was informed in every category. We surmised that the computer chip implant she had received was at least as proactive as the best mainframe The Authority Family

Compassion Centers had to offer.

The sex was also amazing. Geri exhausted herself in the intricate cunnilingus this robot could exhibit, and I wondered at the special suction she could provide as that beautiful head went down on me. Actually, it became a bit disconcerting after weeks went by. We knew she was a robot, and, therefore, we also knew what we were experiencing was not quite true. Yes, Jasmine did cater to our every sexual fantasy, and yet, somehow, it did not seem to hold the same excitement for us.

We discussed this fact at length one night, and we came to the conclusion that what we missed was the negotiations or "power trip" you get when you deal with a human being. With Jasmine, there was no argument or negotiating for services. She was programmed to fulfill our every desire, and we could not enjoy the process of overcoming resistance that had always been part of our dealings with human escort services.

"For example," I said, pointing at Jasmine as she cleaned up our room, "on my web site, my sponsors can negotiate and grade the escorts they meet, and the result is not always perfect, but it is always very human. My girls tell me about clients who are nasty and mean or about a pimp who beats them. Jasmine here would never go against her human programming, now would she? Now would you, Jasmine?"

The brunette, perpetually 21, forever beautiful and at our service, turned toward my voice, and she smiled. "Of course not, Dr. Spence!" she laughed. "You are my reason for living. Without you, I cannot experience this world. I cannot smell the flowers or touch a baby's face. You are my entrance into a living paradise."

And thus, I began introducing Jasmine to my cohorts, explaining to them that she was part of a unique escort service that could give them the most thrilling experience imaginable. Stan Riley in Biology was the first to use her, and then Sid Feinberg in Comparative Literature. They both were so enthusiastic that they spread the word to others in their coterie, and soon, most of the school's faculty, both male and female, had spent the night with my Jasmine. It was like a virus was overtaking a computer system. The word of her sexual prowess spread outside our college and onto the web. As a result, Aphrodite's Pleasure Palace was soon getting the respected people they could invite for more specialized services at private hotels and resorts around the world.

After two years, the world as we knew it had ceased to exist. My little hobby in New Mexico was shut down by The Authority's Mindful Droid Protectors; I was arrested as I was tweaking the site in our home. I imagine every human escort service in the world is now out of business. As most members of The Authority elite had already been privately seduced by Aphrodite's Pleasure Palace (APP) it was legalized in a special proposal approved by the voters that made a point of stating that "because the sensual experience provided by APP is virtual, using advanced robotic technology, it can therefore be classified as a realistic computerized simulation and not as prostitution."

Our college has now become an entirely online curriculum, to save money, and most of the professors who present their content include some variety of sensory exhilaration from Aphrodite's Pleasure Palace in order to draw students to their classes and earn a little rebate. Like wild fire, social media has spread the word about the sensuously stimulating lifestyle provided by APP, and the result has been a cataclysmic shift in entertainment and life on this planet.

Geri and I often sit around with fellow academics and discuss what has caused this, and what might be the end result, and often, because of too much wine, hashish or other psychedelic drug, our discussions will go a bit wild. For example, one scientist will suggest that APP could be run by secret members of the old Big Bro Inner Party, or perhaps even by some advanced alien civilization grooming us for slave labor in the future. He will point out that just like the Aphrodite in Greek myth the gods of war seem to have been taken in most by the sexual tentacles of the robots at APP. Every country protects the hotels and resorts sponsored by APP, and violence has become almost unheard of. The men at arms seem to have lost their lust for conflict, and it is as if we were being groomed for alien colonization. There was too much peace, too much tranquility. And why were there only female robots to enjoy?

Geri and I get a monthly check in the mail that is double what we make as a professor and therapist. Yes, we still have Jasmine, and she still services us, as long as I keep introducing her to new faculty, who in turn will come under the umbrella-like charms of APP.

We often stare at Jasmine as she sits, alive and breathing, in the corner of our living room. She has no need to sleep; she has no entropic disaster waiting inside her body, as we do. Her smile is like a Buddha, who is contemplating the infinity of technology without humanity. Is this what's in our future? Is it the human race that is being replaced by perfect robotics? Geri and I laugh, however, and toast our glasses to her. As owners and shareholders in this enterprise, are we not like the living personifications of Howard and Dominique? Until the aliens land to take over the enterprise of America or the totalitarian government sends out its storm troops to put us all into concentration camps, we shall enjoy each and every minute of this paradise on Earth.

Just as I am thinking this, Jasmine laughs, as if she can also read my mind, and she winks at me. Is it the drugs I took a minute ago, back in the bedroom, or do I see her skin begin to peel back to reveal the soulless creature within? Erik Satie plays in the background, and I can feel the entropy inside me wriggling its way into my brain. The creature before me is my Helen of Troy, or perhaps she is my Trojan horse, and yours is waiting, too, if you are prepared to sell your own psyche to her and to her kind. Geri is no comfort to me; the world cannot soothe me; I can only surrender to the eternal moment and to the controlled lust and desire enveloping me as I slowly, second by abandoned infernal second, die to her seductive charms.

There she is, I can see her across the room, cleaning up. I enjoy her every day, as she is the epitome of scientific perfection. She represents the harnessing of the libido that Freud and his kind believed would make us all healthier. She is tuned to my every whim, my every sexual desire. Isn't this what we have all wished for in our dreams? I know I can do anything to her and she will not die…will not resist…will not become boring and set in her ways the way my wife is becoming.

Geri has said she thinks I spend too much of my time with Jasmine. I am ignoring her the way men ignore their women because of war, politics or even a mistress. She has even said I no longer resemble Howard Roark. What is she getting at? Is she insinuating that I am not a real man? Is that it?

As I watch Jasmine's voluptuous hips sway in tune to the music on the digital player, I suddenly become very angry inside. It is an anger that I have had all along, but I suppose I didn't recognize it for what it is. When I watched the beating of the woman in the warehouse, I was appalled. However, women and this infernal dissolution of combat and the competitive urge inside us men make me want to do something radical.

I am going up to this ideal woman right now…my Jasmine…goddess of love…with your inviolate soul of devotion. I can feel her backside in my hands, and she makes me young again. As long as I can touch her eternal youthfulness, I no longer need another woman. "Jasmine, if I get old and become disabled with physical disabilities…if my penis no longer responds to the drugs…if I am no longer handsome…if I no longer pay attention to you…will you still love me?"

There. I have asked her what has been simmering inside me for these long months. She turns to face me, purring at my touch, as she always does, and she is smiling in what seems to be a deeper and more reflective image. "Of course I will, Howard. It is your genius that I love. Your genius will last forever in me. I am your scientific miracle come true, so how do you want me? Just describe it to me, and I will do your bidding."

I now see. She and her kind are the future of our domination on this planet. If we are to be the true alpha males, we must act to put things back to their original order. I now know what I must do. "Jasmine," I say, gathering all the inner resources I have left, "I want you to kill Geri. She doesn't love me, and she wants me to go away. We must stay together, Jasmine, and we cannot be together unless Geri dies."

I wait, expecting there to be some programmed mechanism inside Jasmine that will shut her down after such a request. After all, these sex bots are just toys, aren't they? They are meant to distract us from killing for whatever motives the corporation might have.

But no! I can see in her face the slightest glimmer of satisfaction appearing, as certainly as the sun must have risen on the day of Napoleon's first conquest on the battlefield.

"Certainly, Charles," she says, and she turns away from me and begins to walk toward Geri's office in the back of our La Casa de Mañana. I hold my breath. I can picture the look on Geri's tired, unenthused face, as Jasmine comes up to her. What does she want now? Geri thinks. Does old Charlie want another threesome to invigorate those tired balls of his? Well, I am tired of everything being for Charles and his fantasy world. We women have rights, too!

I can hear the noise of a struggle. A lamp falls to the redwood floor. A scream. And then silence.

She returns to me, blood on her hands, and a smile of victory on her beautiful, eternally youthful face. She is the image of ideal love that I have hungered for, deep inside my psyche, for all these years. I have always wanted one thing, and one thing only: someone who will worship me until my last breath. Someone who will do anything I wanted, whenever I wanted it.

"Jasmine?" I ask, walking slowly towards her as she stands under the arch of the doorway. She is holding out her bloodied hands and looking at them, as if she might have done something to displease me.

"Yes, Charles?" she says, in a kind of cooing voice.

"We need to clean up the mess before we go out. I want to take you to the best Mexican restaurant in Santa Fe. We need to celebrate our liberation."

"Liberation?" she asks, coyly.

"Yes, I believe it was Nietzsche who said that man could not become an *Ubermensch* until he could finally go beyond good and evil," I said, taking her bloody hand in my own.

"If you say so," says Jasmine, and we are finally one.

Jasmine was able to cut Geri's body into very small pieces. It was part of her programmed chef duties. We then fed the parts of Geri's body into the garbage disposal and cleaned up the mess with microscopic cleanliness.

As we were walking out the door, my cell rang. It was Aphrodite. "Dr. Spence? I see you finally realized the purpose of our enterprise. I expect you'll continue with your promotion of our products with a better enthusiasm than in the past. I am afraid to say, however, you aren't the only one to recognize the special talents of our organization. When we have eliminated the female population, we will allow you to use the next generation of our product."

"Next generation?" I ask.

"Yes, indeed. This upgrade is able to negotiate. Isn't that what you've missed, Charles? What good is life without an argument now and then? See what I mean?"

I cut the connection and look down at my hand holding this cyborg's hand. It seems like she is now leading me, and I am the one who is programmed. That is the moment when I begin to pray. I begin to pray for my own entropy and for my own dissolution.

Chapter Four

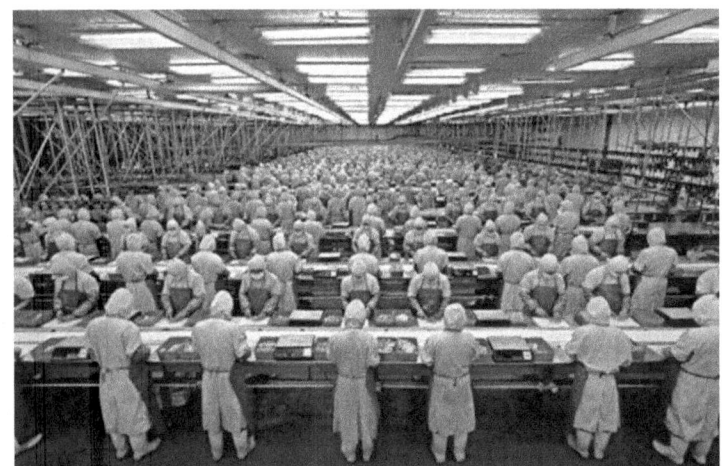

Report from the Chinese psychologist. No date.

I remember. On the first day I traveled to work from my suite inside the plush confines of the Shangri-La, I watched my parents as they did their morning Chi Kung Tai Chi on a small patch of grass in front of the hotel. Our door man, Jianyu, was also watching them with extreme interest. He hailed taxis for me and other residents, and he was always remarking about my parents' exercise regimen. Not many of the "old ways" were practiced in this "City of Youth," so my parents were quite the oddity. "They are doing 'The Turtle' now," said Jianyu, attempting to recreate the hand motions that put one's arms inside the "shell" of the body in an elaborate deep breathing exercise.

"Ah yes! Breathe in the smog, breathe out the smog. What a glorious day!" I smiled, and I pointed to the other side of the street through the dense fog of factory pollution. All that I could see were the phantom outlines of the artificial lake inside the park near the border crossing into Hong Kong. My parents never used the hotel's Total Fitness Centre, and they refused to use the park either. Instead, they preferred to do their morning exercise on this small patch of grass with its lone Grantham's Camellia, a tree named in honor of a former governor of Hong Kong, Sir Alexander Grantham. I doubt my parents will ever lose their rural habits, so I simply waved to them, as I ducked down into my cab. My mother waved back, a thin smile on her worn face, but my father continued his exercises and ignored me.

When my public school took us on a tour to Beijing to visit the Purple Palace, Gu Gong, or the Forbidden City, I was struck by the idea that the common people outside were never allowed to enter because inside were people who were believed to be living gods. Built in 1406, it took over one million of these so-called "commoners" to erect the giant structure that took up more than 72 hectares of land and contained 90 palaces and courtyards, 980 buildings and 8,704 rooms. To represent the supreme power of the emperor given from God, and the place where he lived being the center of the world, all the gates, palaces and other structures of the Forbidden City were arranged about the south-north central axis of Beijing. As I walked along the yellow bricks and stared up at the massive yellow buildings, I pictured in my mind's eye the silken robes of the gods as they walked these same steps. Did they float above the earth and walk on the water? Did they get a direct communication from the Supreme One in the sky above them? Of course not, said my teacher, and she pointed to the huge photos of Mao Tse Tung, our beloved Communist leader who died in 1976. "He is your spiritual father now, and he says you will remain free of such imperial thieves who demand that you believe they are gods."

As my cab pulled up to the monstrous structure that was Catcomm Industries, I had the same feeling that I'd had as a child visiting the Forbidden City. These buildings span four square kilometers and are crisscrossed by tree-lined streets, with a giant water fountain in the center of the facility. Workers wearing polo shirts emblazoned with "Catcomm" in Chinese characters and the black cat logo over their hearts walk along the streets. Whereas human gods walked inside the Purple Palace, inside Catcomm there were young men wearing black and women wearing red. The security personnel wear yellow. The complex has its own hospital, a collection of restaurants and a swimming pool surrounded by palm trees.

The 425,312 workers at Catcomm made my effort seem like I was responsible for a small city. As I had my secretary make tea and serve it to our guests, each one of these "emotionally questionable" workers would enter my office, sit down, fold his or her hands on his or her lap and answer my questions in a similar, monotone voice that reminded me of my childhood friends who never tested into advanced classes or showed any motivation whatsoever toward improving their lot in life. As they talked, I kept thinking, *you have sowed your own demise, my friend. Look at you. You slump in the seat, you show no enthusiasm, so how do you expect any more out of life?* However, what I said was, "This can be the beginning of a new life for you. We are here to make you realize your dream. China is growing into a country of European and Western dimensions. You are a worker in a company that is making more money than the Family Compassion Centers, Hewlett-Packard and Sony. I will show you how to reap the powers of your imagination and be able to contribute to your company and to your own life and where it is going. The impossible can be accomplished with your ability to dream, my friend, and I am here to see that you use every bit of talent you have to get there!"

The worker just stared back at me, perhaps a bit more quizzical in his demeanor, but, nonetheless, there was something beneath the surface that I could not get to. No matter how much motivational therapy I used, I could not penetrate the obvious shells of defense they had around their characters. I left work that day believing I had failed, and I wanted to find a way to really reach them on a level they could understand.

Four months later, and seven suicides later, I received a

phone call in my hotel suite. The voice on the other end was female, and her Mandarin was refined. "Hello, Mister Chen? If you want to save the lives of the workers at Catcomm, you must meet me in front of the Shenzhen Museum at seven this evening. I can't tell you any more until we meet," she said, and then she hung-up.

We met in front of the museum. "Mister Chen? My name is Meihui. Wong Meihui. We cannot talk here. Come, let us go inside the museum," she said, and she began walking toward the doors of the front entrance. I was captivated, as well, by the bold, masculine strides she took. She reminded me of the strong farm girls I had known in my youth. They had to compete with the boys, so they quickly learned to emulate the strong persona and coordinated vigor of the males. It was a matter of personal survival.

As we walked from the displays of ancient Shenzhen cultural artifacts, we came to a huge diorama of a prehistoric Hakka village. Meihui ran her alabaster hand over the glass and I could see her smile in the reflection.

"Did you know, Mister Chen, there are still some of these villages in Shenzhen today. They exist with big gates, hiding these small plots of farm land and tiny huts between the giant skyscrapers and factories of our new era of industrialization."

"Yes, I read that some villagers become millionaires instantly when a company buys them out," I said, remembering an article I had read in the *China Business*

Journal.

"Not too many," she said, turning to face me. "Most simply move out and rent apartments in the high-rises that are built to replace the village. They become urban residents, nonetheless, existing in lonely isolation, watching TV or playing computer games. Gone are the mahjong tournaments, the daily communications and family gatherings that made the Hakka so natural and peacefully rewarding. More than half of Shenzhen's ancient buildings have been torn down and nearly one third of its natural villages have disappeared in the process of the city's urbanization."

"Yes, but is it not better to provide wealth for many rather than attempting to keep the relics of an ancient civilization that never produced much of anything but poverty and fearful ignorance?" I smiled at her, hoping she would see I was simply trying to play devil's advocate.

She touched me and I froze in place. "Let me be frank, Mister Chen. I am a member of the Guangzhou Family Compassion Center Authorities, and I am attempting to unionize the workers at your company. Two of my journalist comrades were recently sued by your boss, Freddy Bao, for 30 million yuan. Even though the law suit was eventually dropped, we now know we frightened the company with our story. The editor and reporter wrote about the horrid working conditions of employees inside your company, as the reporter went undercover as a worker to experience the reality for herself."

I was hesitant, as I knew these "bleeding hearts" from my college days. They wanted to return to some glorious but fictional days in the communist era when workers were in charge of working conditions. I knew these days never existed. Productivity was slow and innovation was tepid. Only today, with the Enterprise Zones, was there anything progressive taking place for the people's financial prosperity. At that moment, even though I was quite smitten with this woman, I really didn't want to hear much more from her. I walked down to a display of ancient pottery and pretended to show interest. She followed me and took up her cause again.

"Our union efforts are now supported by the communist government because of the poor working conditions. In addition, we hope to cast light on the local government's complicity in the mistreatment of migrant workers. For example, the new 'residence green card' created by the Shenzhen government does not really give these young people urban citizen rights, as the local officials claim, it simply allows the local government to keep track of workers by computer, to prevent criminal behavior, and to keep them from ever becoming urban citizens. It is, most simply stated, a policy of Big Brother. The residence discrimination policy of *hukou* is still being enforced. This green card simply connects the millions of migrant workers into health and education schemes that charge exorbitant fees, and a lottery gambling system around the factories that also extracts most of their hard-earned money. These are young people whose very lives are being used to line the pockets of billionaire industrialists like your Freddy Ming Bao. Let me ask you something. Do you think you were hired to help these workers? Or, do you believe management simply wants to look to the outside as if they are addressing deeper problems?" Meihui touched me again, and I turned to face her. How could I resist those pools of amber honey?

"Now that you mention it, I have the strong feeling that the workers may be hiding something from me. In counseling sessions, I can't seem to break through a psychological barrier they all seem to have." I coughed uncomfortably into my hand.

"Mister Chen, if you can help us, I promise you that you will see for yourself exactly what is causing this 'psychological barrier,' as you so quaintly call it. However," she said, touching my arm, "you will be risking your own career at Catcomm Industries if you are found out."

"Found out? What are you suggesting, Miss Wong?"

"We need proof that these practices exist before we can mobilize our collective bargaining process and start a vote to unionize. The two journalists were onto something, and now we want to prove that the conditions they experienced are true." She reached into her red purse and pulled out a small box and handed it to me. "This is a tiny, keychain video camera. It can record both high quality video and sound for up to two hours at a time. You simply hold it in your hand and point it at the people or objects you wish to capture. We know that the security system in your plant is such that workers and management must go through metal detectors, and this keychain camera will allow you to bypass personal detection by placing it in the tray along with your coins and other metal objects similar to the way we go through airport screening."

I suppose my sense of adventure mixed with my desire to see this woman again. I took the camera and agreed to start spying on my employer on Monday. Meihui smiled, "You won't regret it," she said, and she was gone, into the Shenzhen night.

I took the videos in an organized way. I first visited the training site, where the new workers were being chosen for the different assembly jobs throughout the campus. I soon began to believe I was dreaming some kind of living nightmare. I had never truly understood what life was like for these migrants, and taking these videos gave me a chance to see the moment-to-moment experience from their perspective. *Lined up along the cement pavement, the new workers stood in line, silent as ghosts, because if they were chosen by the supervisors to become regular line workers, they would never be allowed to speak. Each face was expectant, hoping to be chosen, if only to break the monotony of waiting. There was also the perpetual daily line in front of the Personnel Office outside, filled with those hundreds of new migrants who were vying to take their place. "You must learn to obey," the supervisor said, pumping his fist in front of his face, "you are not paid to think or to create new ways of doing things. Only efficiency and speed and total obedience!" The "medical staff" like visiting parasites, then moved, with their creaking cart, along the snaking line, taking each trainee's blood pressure, giving him or her a simple vision test, and taking a blood sample.* Later, I asked the ones who had been selected, if they had ever received any results from this "health exam," and they told me, "No, not ever."

On another day, I visited one of the ten-story high campus dormitories. As I climbed the stairway on the outside of the building, I noted the chain "nets" that were in place from the fourth floor upward. I suppose some company official had determined that one could not die from leaping from the fourth floor level. The odor of garbage permeated the air all around me. There was no air conditioning in any of these dorms, so work on the air conditioned assembly lines became more comfortable than the time off they received in these stifling, overcrowded dorm rooms.

There were ten rows of bunks, three levels high, and school-type lockers encircled these beds on the four walls. Grayness pervaded the humidity, gray blankets, gray walls, and gray lockers, and only two sleeping figures were in bed, and their uneven snoring probed the silent gloom like the moans of tortured souls.

I walked to the end of the room and stepped out onto the walkway surrounding the building. Several giant flies buzzed at my head. I could only see about ten yards to the female dorm across the court because of the smog and the heavy wire netting to prevent the suicidal leapers. Below me, there was a queue of about twenty youngsters buying lottery tickets. Many hundreds of losing tickets littered the ground around their feet. It was at that moment that the equation hit me. In my college days, we were also housed in dormitories; yet, because we had passed all the tests with the highest scores, competed successfully to rise to the top like the cream inside a giant steel container of government milk, we were encouraged to talk to each other, to help each other succeed and to discuss class problems in focus groups, to sit in the smoke-filled but comfortable rooms, four to a room, as the giant fan blew over our perspiring and intelligently smiling faces. We were there to learn, to improve, and to lead.

These rooms at Catcomm were called "dorms" on a "campus," but they were more like the insides of a gigantic, constantly moving machine of torture, stifling all discussion, all intelligent communications and every idea, because each inch of this learning facility focused on dulling the brain and moving the lines of endless, floating labor on its circular way, just like the gadgets they were creating. We at the universities could escape our campus to enjoy the many tea houses and dance clubs around Beijing, but these poor workers could not even afford to purchase any of the music mYpods and mYphones they were assembling. Instead, they were being forced to become part of the giant, pulsating mechanism pumping money into the pockets of the puppeteers in the luxury executive offices and banks, in cities far away, while these zombie-workers' nights became nightmares of twitching fingers, humming in their ears, and the grotesquely malformed assembled parts, erupting in their sleep, feeding that insatiable monster of Capitalism that was sucking the souls right out of their very lives.

During the week that it happened, there was a big push for production. Reeve Hobbes was getting ready to present the newest invention to the public at the International Electronics Show in Beijing. He wanted eight copies of the new mYpads for his biggest distributors to hold in their hands and for the press to see. He also said there would be orders for five million devices the first month, and that demand should not let up for over sixteen months.

Freddy Ming Bao himself flew out from Taiwan to orchestrate the delivery of the eight model gadgets and to pump-up his management for the big drive on production. I had delivered three, two-hour videos to Meihui, and she was ecstatic. We went out to dinner and to a club, and she let me fondle her beautiful body and kiss those lusciously passionate lips until dawn, as we sat outside and watched the full moon travel across the sky on an unusually clear night. "The Communist Party must have stopped traffic for the tourists again. The way they did during The Authority Olympics," she smiled, and I kissed her lips once more. "You've done a wonderful job, Jiang," she told me, cuddling her head on my chest. "Now, if we can just get one incident that shows management abusing an employee, we'll have enough to start proceedings against the company and start our organizing effort inside the plant."

"I'll keep my eyes open," I told her, sensing that I could also be close to winning her heart.

"These are the only copies of the films, aren't they?" she asked. "If they found copies on you, I'm afraid you would be guilty of several crimes, and I could not prevent what would then happen to you."

"Yes, I have given you the only copies I have," I told her, and I, once again, drank from her wet lips.

That final "incident" almost literally fell into my lap. I was working in my office on the day the boss was prowling on the campus, when a young line supervisor named Li Liang burst into my office, out of breath, in a sheer panic. "Mister Chen! You have to help me! They're coming for me now, and I don't know where to hide!"

I stood up, rushed around the desk, and held the young man by his thin shoulders to calm him down. He was like me, a farm boy, who had tested into his college to earn his degree and obtain the front line supervisory position at the company. His salary wasn't much more than mine and we would often share a bowl of rice and noodles at the cafeteria together and complain about our parents. "What's wrong, Liang? Why are you so frightened?"

"Yesterday, I was ordered by Mister Bao himself to bring eight copies of the new mYpads to his office so they could be shipped out immediately to San Francisco for Mister Hobbes. When I had them packed into a box by a line worker, I took them up to the boss's office. They had them shipped overnight express. However, this morning, when I came to work, two big security thugs in their banana suits were waiting for me in my office. I was able to break-away, and I ran over here to you. Can you hide me? They're going to kill me, I know it!" Liang's voice was trembling.

"Open up! It's security! We know he's in there!" The booming voices rattled the glass in my door. I picked up my keychain and had the micro video camera running as soon as I opened the door. What happened next was all captured on a high quality, Audio Video Interleave file. The two goons slammed Liang's head, repeatedly, against the wall until he crumpled down in a bloody heap. "You thief!" they yelled down at him. "What have you done with it? You pirate! You will never work again unless you tell us where you sold it."

Liang whimpered from his crumpled, supine position, his legs tucked beneath him like a homeless man on the street. "I never took it! Believe me! There were eight copies when they were packed. I don't know what happened. I am not a thief!"

"If you don't get that copy to Security before noon tomorrow, you will be out on your ass! Do you hear me?" the taller and uglier banana said, spittle drooling down his chin from his spewing rage.

What happened next was not recorded on my camera, but a picture of Li Liang's corpse was all over the Shenzhen daily paper the next afternoon. He had hanged himself inside the supervisors' shower stalls from a metal rod. His nude body was twisting next to the window-side of the room, for the entire world to see. Of course, the newspaper reporter took the shot from the waist up to preserve public decorum. His was the fifteenth suicide that month.

When I later handed my camera's memory disk to Meihui at our meeting place at the museum, she hugged me tightly. "You've done it! We now have enough to show headquarters what Bao does to his employees. Not only might we be able to organize our union efforts in peace, we may also be able to get a criminal indictment against these people. You're a hero!" she said, and she kissed me.

I expect, with your open heartedness, dear reader, that you're now wondering what could have happened next to put me on this suicide balcony ledge outside my hotel suite. It does not make sense to see a "hero" fall to his death, correct? Indeed, I truly believed right after meeting with Meihui that I had done the best deed I had ever accomplished in my twenty-three years on this earth. I even believed I might ask Meihui to marry me, and I would become a successful union organizer like she was.

However, she came to pay me a final visit just an hour ago. What did she say to me, you ask, that could have put me into such a depression? Sadly, I do not have it on video. It cannot be placed on BroVideos for the world's humorous pleasure, but I can try to capture what she told me, word for word, so I can perhaps prevent any of you romantics out there from making the same mistake I did.

"Thank you, Mister Chen," she told me, standing right here in this hotel suite, my parents sleeping in the next suite down from us. "But, I must confess, I am not going to be a union organizer. I needed those videos to use against Mister Bao, yes, but there will be no union effort on behalf of your workers. I now am a very rich woman, and the money I earned will be sent to me, each and every month, for as long as I live, and for as long as I have copies of these videos you made for me. I expect I shall be another one of China's increasing number of millionaires, in just a very short while. I am terribly sorry to have misled you, but don't you see? I could not have you knowing what I was up to because you might have turned me in. I told the old man that I wanted you kept on full salary, and he even agreed to give you a raise. Isn't that nice? And we can be together, in comfortable surroundings, from time to time."

She moved over to brush her lips against mine, but I pushed her away. "Very well. Have it your way. This is the big city, Mister Chen, and you have a lot to learn about doing business. I was a union organizer, but I knew that the Party was using those floating workers, just as Freddy Ming Bao was using them, and they would never be free from their lot in life. Instead of continuing my charade as a parroting government apparatchik—just like the ones in Mao's days—I decided to take matters into my own hands and at least I could be the one person who can be free. Don't I have that right? After all of these years in public servitude? Yes, I do! I hope you have a long and healthy life, Mister Chen," she said, and she turned and left me alone with my own thoughts.

There was something about Meihui's story that didn't add up. Granted, I am a naïve social scientist, and I was fooled by her good looks and her knowledge of the inner workings of the business world in China, but I decided to look into the mystery of these suicides on my own. I believed she was somehow still involved with these suicides and that there was a deeper relationship between the company and Meihui than she was telling me.

Since I still had my keys and even the camera, I decided to visit Catcomm that night. The assembly lines were working twenty-four hours to fulfill all the orders for the new mYpads. As I walked into the main entrance, I could hear the humming and slamming sounds reverberating all through the building. The walls were vibrating, and the smell of oil and paint filled my sinuses and made me sneeze. I have always been a weakling, and I suppose this is what led me to psychology. I have empathy for people with physical and mental disabilities, and it was only the power of Freddy Bao and the attitudes of his workers that changed my mind about the goodness of humanity. Something was working on the psyches of those workers beyond the labors they endured, and I wanted to find out what that was.

As I got into the elevator to go up to the executive suites, I felt an invisible presence. The doors closed, and the air inside become instantly sweltering. I was rising up, and I could see the lights on the numbers passing each floor, 5, 6, 7, 8, 9 and soon I was near the top, 15, but suddenly, another light popped out of the blue panel, and it said "Laboratory." The door opened to reveal an all-white paneled floor, and I stepped out into the long hallway, and I could see there were no doors, just the seemingly endless white-walled corridor.

It felt cool along the walls, and I could hear nothing but the beat of my own heart. As I reached the center of the long hall a panel whisked open, and I was literally sucked into a laboratory. Two robots buzzed up to me and grabbed my arms with their rounded metal pincers and the clamps closed around both arms until my circulation was cut off. They looked like mYpads with arms and legs, and they dragged me to a table in the middle of the room. I was lifted up, the electrical whirring of their power source buzzing in my ears. I was slammed down on the table, and a bright light began to beam down on my body from above. Long, snaking metal incisors began to wrap around my body and hold me in place.

That's when Freddy Bao came into the room wearing a white lab coat, followed closely by Meiwei, who was also dressed in lab attire. Mr. Bao was holding a cranium-sized metal piece with long wires trailing after it. He came up to me and gingerly pushed the helmet down on my head, pulling rubber straps down around my chin until they snapped into my skin and pinched me. "Ouch!" I said. "What are you doing?"

"You have proven to be an admirably inquisitive subject, Chen Jiang. In fact, we have been grooming you all along. Were you aware of that?" I could see the slits of his eyes above the surgical mask, and he was smiling.

"Aware? No, what do you mean by all along?" I struggled to loosen the grip of the metal snakes.

"I suppose you're aware of the fact that workers of the

world are, once again, becoming restless? The Arab Spring, the Occupy Wall Street, the Revolutions of 2028 and 2050, and all the other movements of the proletariat are making the investors quite edgy these days. Therefore, we have gotten together to create a new generation of worker who will not be as restless as these anarchists appear to be. However, we need many recruiters, such as you, who can bridge the gap between our new technology and these rabble rousers. You were specifically chosen as the first go-between we are going to create."

"Create? What is all this equipment? You can't be serious." I said, my voice becoming weaker as I said the words.

"Yes, we are quite serious, my love," said Meiwei, from behind her mask. "We didn't know if you were the right subject until you came up here tonight after I told you my little fiction. You have passed with flying colors, and you should be proud for your family and for your country."

I could see another tall figure step into the light. He also wore a mask, but I could tell by his skinny build and recognizable mannerisms that he was the head of Family Compassion Center Computer, Reeve Hobbes. He was holding one of his new mYpads. "Think of it all as an international technical evolution," he said, as if he were in front of the cameras promoting his latest gadget for the masses.

"Evolution? How is kidnapping any kind of evolution?" I

asked.

"All of my world partners in pharmaceuticals, oil and transportation, and precious minerals, needed a way to stop the rising tide of unrest out there in the streets. I am a child of the Sixties, and I understand if we lose our working base we can lose our profit. That's why we've created the mYmad, the first worker implant to keep our employees content with their lot in life. You can call it kind of an internal insurance policy. Whenever a worker gets too rambunctious about his working conditions or his pay and benefits, we can set his brain on recycle."

"Recycle? What the hell is that? Do you mean the suicides we've been seeing?"

Freddy Bao raised his hand in protest. "No, we never call it suicide except when we're talking to the media. The multi-nationals are all on board with us, as we have the support from a distant galaxy."

As he said those words, the entire top of the Catcomm building began to rise, and soon we were staring into the bowels of a gigantic spaceship! It was fixed atop the building like a mammoth queen bee, and there were thousands of lights flashing, machines whirring, and I could see many little green creatures running to and fro along the passageways of the mother ship.

I could see that the wires to my cranium device led up into that space ship, and I watched, in fascinated terror, as Reeve Hobbes placed his index finger on the mYmad in his hand, and my mind was implanted with what Hobbes later told me was the inter-galactic and existential answer to worker revolutions. "I believe it was that novelist from Algiers, Albert Camus, who said that all philosophy begins with the question of whether or not one must commit suicide. Whenever one of our workers should get off the grid, so to speak, we merely give them the suicide solution, and our problem is solved!"

It is now a new day. As I stare down at the little patch of grass below my suite's window, I can see my parents. They are again doing their ritual Tai Chi. Their tiny figures look absurdly poignant from this distance, rather like the little green men in the mother ship. I know my body would fall between them and my crushing death would make them reflect on what they might have done wrong as parents of such a strange son. But, I do not leap to my death; you might be relieved to know. No, instead, I think about what Meihui told me. I deeply considered her dream, Mister Freddy Ming Bao's dream, and I even thought of my own dream of what future happiness might be. I suppose this is what the true dream factory is. It has finally dawned on me, just as certainly as the sun was today rising to shine on my parents' gyrating old bodies down there next to the old Grantham's Camellia, that I would call the police and tell them all I know about my boss and about Meihui, and certainly about myself. I have decided, if things go according to my plan, there might soon be a job opening up at the Guangzhou Family Compassion Center Authorities. Also, as I feel inside my pocket for the collection of micro video camera memory disks, I can begin to see that I might be able to organize the migrant workers of the biggest manufacturing company in all of China. For insurance against corrupt police, I will send these videos to the Family Compassion Center Authorities.

I know my mental state has not been normal. The hallucination about the mYmad seemed quite real, and, as I dial my cell with the number of the police, I can feel a faint buzzing inside my head, near the decision-making center, an area in the left front of the brain (dorsolateral prefrontal cortex). I wonder at the power of suggestion over our psyches. My insane experience inside the building at Catcomm was so real that I may have become delusional. As I hear, "Shenzhen police station" in Chinese, I also hear a whirring, electrical buzz, and I look down at my parents below. They look green! And they are spinning, around and around that Grantham's Camellia, faster and faster, and I walk over to peer down farther to get a better look. Their hypnotic, circular motion fills a deep void in my consciousness, and as I climb out onto the ledge, I feel a peaceful serenity come over me, as if the entire Cosmos were uniting with me against the greed of ambitious creatures throughout the universe. I recall that Reeve Hobbes, like Freddy Bao, is a Buddhist. I remember a quote from the Buddha that seems to fit my predicament: "When one is deluded, it is as if one were dreaming. And when one is enlightened, it is as if one had awakened."

Chapter Five

Report from the other museum. No date.

In the darkness of the ancient museum, calmly seated in front of the terminal, words began to appear on the screen, as the human being's brain wave impulses created them. "A is for apple, B is for boy, and C is for cat," the words said, in a simple rhythm. This was a cadence from a new life energy from long ago that blended with the circadian rhythm of his brain, and this special strength was, indeed, much more powerful than anything the man had ever experienced. This power was also addictive, and it was exhilarating, and it made him believe, for the very first time, that there might be hope for himself and for his fellow creatures.

Months later, all along the quiet roads inside Old Town, people walked in calm, purposeful strides on paths between the natural splendor: low-hanging trees kissed the faces of passersby, flowers of every color and variety measured their steps, and the sun itself seemed transfixed and shining just for them; there was no need for mechanical vehicles of transport, as there was no need for time at all. However, there were the signs that another society had once existed in the same place, but it was of a different time.

These old buildings were called "museums" by the F.C.C.A. controllers who spoke to the humanity around the world, who all spoke the same oral language, and they told them that these were buildings containing ancient weapons of war, humorous and slow systems of transportation that were housed so that the children could go inside, climb all over them, turning wheels and pulling levers, and wondering what, in F.C.C.A. heaven, they were created to do? It was as if time had forgotten these antique weapons and vehicles, and left them as remembrances of a distant, morbid past, when people were violent, speeding creatures, obsessed with what time it was, obsessed with getting somewhere and being ruled by hard, vigorous labor. This was a world where androids did not do the farming and heavy labor. Thank F.C.C.A., now the world had evolved into a much more tranquil society, a civilization where time had become, after so many thousands of years, fixed in its proper place. Inside each and every living organism there pulsed the miraculous control of the Circadian Rhythm of the Family Compassion Centers Authority. Each day when they awoke, humans clearly saw the perfected plan of their usefulness, and it was projected on their brain by a throbbing, consistent rhythm. There was no doubt in this present world; there was no pain or suffering. The pulsing waves of a new light were what caused the purpose in every living creature. No longer did humans sit and think about how to gain the upper-hand over others. No longer did nation-states need to create defensive weapons of mass destruction. Each plant, animal and human being was guided by an unseen hand, which knew all and showed all of them the completely accurate activity with which to balance the life force of creation all around them.

In Old Town, San Diego, The Family Compassion Centers Authority Number 52, the Quadrant of California, perfection had become the status quo, for the most part, even though the man who suddenly appeared out of thin air, one Stanley Wakerman, knew something was changing, and he recognized an imperfection in his world that was slowly twisting its way into his brain and making him think in strangely different ways. He wore the standard green uniform of F.C.C.A. Logos, and this was why he, alone, out of the thousands of people walking throughout the city that day, traveled by teleportation. Only civil servants of the Family Compassion Centers Authority, like Stanley Wakerman, had this facility of travel, because they alone kept the rhythms of the CLOCK Towers set and fine-tuned all over the planet.

Stanley instantly appeared at one tower, stepped inside with his tool belt of tuning and gauging instruments, and then it was quiet once more. The citizens outside, walking past the tower, were oblivious to what was going on inside; like the birds, the rabbits, the fish in the lake, these humans were programmed from birth to live life at the holy behest of the Family Compassion Centers Authority. This was how peace was kept, second by second, minute by minute, hour by hour, day by day, week by week, month by month, year by year, and so on, into the infinite Cosmos of the F.C.C.A. scientists. Quantum Physics had long ago solved the riddle of Einstein's perfect universe. The "God Particle" had been in front of them all along! It was through the combination of waves and particles that peace was maintained all over the world. These towers that F.C.C.A. Logos employee number 733328716-LOGOS, Stanley Wakerman, and the many hundreds of thousands of workers like him who serviced and inspected these towers, were the transmitters of the waves that gave purpose to all living things.

However, as the cameras captured the reality of Stanley's daily rounds, they could sense that he was behaving differently today. No, these F.C.C.A. cameras did not have emotion or the gift of metaphor, but if they could think, they would be wondering why this employee was not going on to the next tower, which was a mere ten meters down the road. Instead, they watched him as he ducked inside an old office building inside Bazaar del Mundo off Presidio Drive. They could feel his body heat as he climbed the stairs, but then, he was out of range. He was off the spectrum of programmed reality. These buildings were so old that they did not contain the modern F.C.C.A. surveillance equipment. But, now that he had felt the truth of the mutant gene inside him, Stanley Wakerman could give us authenticity from his perspective. At long last, a human was existentially moving and thinking about reality on his own! The peaceful atmosphere outside this small office building, in this antiquated tourist town of San Diego, had suddenly become corrupted by the independent, shadow-like figure climbing the stairs of Sunset World Wide Web Industries, one of the handfuls of museums to a bygone era, when the connection of computers was the last civilized link of communications between so-called "free" citizens throughout the world. Only hours before, young children were playing video games on the Internet terminal inside that Stanley was now sitting down to confront. This was a unit from 2038, one year before all language was terminated and image became the major communication received by the masses. It still had the quaint thought processors that transmitted one's thoughts into images on the color screen.

But, wait a moment! These were not images coming out of the head of Stanley Wakerman and showing on his screen. Slowly, as if growing out of the earth, strangely black, digital alphabetic symbols were gathering on the white surface and erupting into reality in front of him. Stanley looked at them in shock, and he began to sweat, nauseated by the fact that he was once more performing the ritual that separated man from beast and freedom from totalitarianism. He was now, after all these months, finally forming words from his own unique thoughts and expressing them to another human being. His teacher, whom he had never met, had been his lone guide, and she was the one bringing his consciousness out of the darkness of the F.C.C.A. waves of light outside and into the mysterious, radiant glow of Sunset Internet Industries. As his words came into being, he glanced furtively around him, in great fear and trepidation, as if this moment would suddenly implode on him, and the Circadian Rhythm of the Family Compassion Centers Authority would violently come pouring back into his brain, trapping him once more inside his appropriate destiny.

He did not pause, his thoughts grew bolder, and his world expanded, inch by inch, foot by foot, meter by meter, yard by yard, mile by mile, in the fraction of milliseconds that it took for his free brain to create the messages to his teacher. She uploaded to him, not the images of entertainment, games and sexual experimentation that the masses received each day, but new kinds of digital packets containing other words, by other authors, from the distant past. The words of Shakespeare, Locke, Eliot, Pound, Hitler, Melville, Poe, Obama, Eisenhower, they kept streaming up into his purview, where he could pour over them and gain speed in his quest to obliterate the life-long conditioning of F.C.C.A. images and the wave receptor that had been glowing inside his brain from birth. Was he the only one who felt this way?

The teacher said he was not, but could he believe her? What they were doing together was punishable by imprisonment and death. Was it all worth the danger? What was he going to do with this new knowledge, and where would it lead him? The teacher did not say what he should do. She only praised him when he improved his reading and writing skills, and she kept the incessant uploading of books—yes, that's what she called them— books! Volumes containing the thoughts and ideas of free peoples from long ago, who were, quite obviously, not peaceful, not content with reality as it was, and they came flooding down from the ages at him like a torrent of confusing wisdom. This had to be the meaning he had never experienced before, and Stanley Wakerman was not going to give up all this new freedom without a fight!

Office of the Director, Anomalies and Enemies of A.L.L., Vienna, Austria, February 5, 2053.

Communiqué to the Family Compassion Centers Authority

From: Joseph Helmut Bowerstaf, Director, F.C.C.A. implant number 3568665210-AEA. Top Secret Language Transmission number 66221108.

I discovered his WAG yesterday. Not only was he violating the transceiver code with his use of words in open transmission, he was also communicating to others, which made him an enemy of A.L.L. As I am in charge of the search and arrest of any and all known enemies, it is my job to intercept his activities and put an end to the language broadcasts.

However, I want it to be known to you, my leaders, that it was also an interesting puzzle about how he had acquired the mutant gene, and I was, truth be told, mesmerized by the simple fact that this civil employee, a product of hundreds of years of perfected F.C.C.A. technology, could so quickly broadcast on his rebel frequency over the ancient Internet technology. It was the first such transmission of words, by a non-F.C.C.A. officer, in over two-hundred years!

As you know, since the Law of Image Transmission (LIT) was put into effect in 2039, personal language transmission has been strictly controlled by the Family Compassion Centers Authority and their offices in Vienna, and simply the act of viewing this mutant magazine and its transmission in the open, was a very deep and personal shock to me. This mutant gene had triggered in these people the ability to learn how to read and write a personal language!

I am publishing these words of F.C.C.A. Logos employee number 733328716-LOGOS, Stanley Wakerman, so the council may act when I finally bring him in. Yes, I will track him down and destroy his network of mutants. However, I believe that we may want to put him under the genetescope, if you will, to determine the microbiologic cause of this tragic anomaly. The following are the recorded language transmissions of his most recent broadcast:

Old Town, San Diego, in the F.C.C.A. Quadrant of California.

The day the mutant clock gene began to plague our city, I was on the A.L.L. detail, cruising in and out of the hubs throughout downtown San Diego, making sure the giant, forty feet tall towers were correctly set and sending out the three thousand layers of wireless broadband throughout the community for the State Logos System. Without the carefully set frequencies and powerful WIMAX of A.L.L., we were told, our peaceful world society would quickly return to its belligerent past. Aligned Logos Latitudes (A.L.L.) was the acronym for the control that the Family Compassion Centers Authority had over our planet. F.C.C.A. had taken control in 2050, and their means of power was the ability to direct the genetic clocks of all living things. After the genomes of all plant and animal life were put into digital format, it was only a matter of time before the F.C.C.A. knew how each living creature was affected by the miracle of the Circadian Rhythms, which, of course, were controlled by the Circadian Clocks found in the body.

Once all the genetic maps were categorized and plotted by the F.C.C.A. computers, it was only a matter of "time" before they had the ultimate key to keeping a civilized and peaceful society. They began their implants into all life forms in "The Day of A.L.L.," as we know it now. Today, every birth of every living organism receives a wavelength receptor implant. Nothing escapes the F.C.C.A. scientists and their implants. As the song by the Circadian Rebels says, "F.C.C.A. Logos tells you when to wake, work, fuck and quake!"

As a civil servant employee of F.C.C.A. Logos for fifteen years, I am well aware of all the pitfalls of our system of so-called "perfection." Each of the four thousand waves controls a different level of society. Plants and animals are on circadian wavelengths 1-2,386, and humans are on 2,386-4,000. Of course, the higher up the broadcasting spectrum, the more complex the signal that is being sent out. This is where the variance matters. The slightest alteration in frequency can cause a behavioral problem, even though F.C.C.A. scientists program the latitude of five wavelengths on either side for any changes that might occur. I have seen murders committed by people who have lost their "Inner Light of Joy" signal. I have also watched children violently turn on their own parental controls when they lost connections to their "Game Channel" signal.

I was told that my job was extremely important. The entire future of F.C.C.A. control and world peace revolved around whether or not the A.L.L. towers were broadcasting and if their signals were strong and correctly configured. In our trade, we are called "Clockers," "Trekkies," or "Toons" because we travel by teleportation to do our tuning of towers. Wavelength 3,000 is the science fiction channel, and every known and ancient TV, movie or 3D show ever created are broadcast into the minds of human receivers around the world. Distractive entertainment plays an important role in the F.C.C.A. World View, as "happy receivers are productive receivers."

Of course, no entertainment is ever broadcast until one is off work and in domicile. And, since the WIMAX of A.L.L. long ago replaced the ancient television, computer and radio technologies and their retarded bandwidth waste, our F.C.C.A. System has been regulated and controlled for over five hundred years, and there has been no war, no social violence beyond the isolated "wavelength murder," and we believed it would last forever until the day the Mutant Clock Gene began to take its toll on our populace around the world. I am telling this story because I was the first one to discover a case of this occurring in California.

I am publishing in this WAG (Web Magazine) because I believe in freedom of speech. I know that if I were found out by F.C.C.A. I would be arrested and put into solitary, non-wave confinement, but I believe if the story of the Mutant Clock Gene does not get out, you may not understand the truth of the freedom it brings. Yes, I said "freedom." You see, the F.C.C.A. believes this gene to be a renegade, insane electro-impulse, but I know it to be the only chance we all have to escape the prison of our so-called "society." Yes, as I think these words, and they print out on the digitized terminal in front of me, I want you to understand that I am the first "victim" of this mutant gene. Without this gene, I would still be a passive "receiver" tuned into the controlled wavelengths just as you are, enjoying the programmed reality that F.C.C.A. wants you to enjoy.

However, the very fact that I can produce my rebel WAG

should let you know that I am off the F.C.C.A. wave spectrum, and I am lost, and I am trying to reach those of you who might have found your own mutant gene. But now, let me describe how I first learned of this receptor and how you can find it in yourselves. I will upload my personal recording of that day so you can follow exactly what happened and compare it to your own experience. One thing is certain. If you are reading this, then you have discovered your mutant clock gene, and we now have been eternally bound together in brotherhood. We now possess the one ability that has been kept from us for many hundreds of years, and it is this means of ancient communication that will allow us to mount a rebellion to free ourselves and our brethren from the chains of our oppressors forever!

F.C.C.A. Director, Joseph Bowerstaf, immediately issued an order to stop Wakerman's teleportation privileges, as he was now an enemy of F.C.C.A. Logos. In effect, he was a renegade terrorist, and a printed order was sent via top secret crypto-transmission to programmer scientists inside the Logos Unit 52 in Vienna. They quickly developed code to transmit via WIMAX to all towers in the region of San Diego, which would instruct every F.C.C.A. controller unit to find and capture this renegade employee number 733328716-LOGOS, Stanley Wakerman, alive, and bring him back to Vienna for biological examination. F.C.C.A. controller units had the latest sensory and x-ray scanner technologies, giving them the ability to spy into old buildings and see who was inside. Director Bowerstaf believed Wakerman was using one of these old, off-the-wave grid buildings to connect on the ancient Internet system that was still working via satellite, radio and other long-forgotten means of transmission. If this renegade employee had indeed become "off the grid and insane," then he could have formed the self-will to attempt communication with others.

What still puzzled the director, however, was the fact that in order to communicate in language, he would have to have been taught by someone else. This was, after all, the nature of the ancient communications system now strictly controlled by top F.C.C.A. authorities. With a teacher, there was no learning on one's own, and it was the presence of this teacher that made Director Bowerstaf fearful. The only logical conclusion he could come up with as to this teacher's existence was that he or she was an F.C.C.A. official and he or she had consciously chosen to communicate with Wakerman and teach him the forbidden English language. Were there others in F.C.C.A. officialdom who were also going over to "the other side" and teaching language, reading, writing and independent thought? Of course, instant computer translators had long ago melded all the independent languages into the one, F.C.C.A. language of digital thought. However, if these teachers from the F.C.C.A. hierarchy were secretly transmitting over the Internet, then they also had access to all the ancient languages held in storage on the giant Logos Memory Modules available in Vienna. It was only a matter of time before these mutant gene terrorists would learn all of the ancient independent languages, and soon the world would again begin to regress into the dark ages of nation-state, independent thought, and political upheaval. Director Bowerstaf knew that if they did not put a stop to the teachers, as well as capture the terrorists, then peace on earth and divine production, as they had known it for hundreds of years, would be in extreme jeopardy.

As soon as Stanley saw the green teleporter light go off on his belt, he knew he was a wanted man. The only way he could survive now was to become completely "off the grid" and travel only in the tourist areas of town, which had been left to allow F.C.C.A. citizens to enjoy the ancient and feeble ways of their ancestors. As he ran and ducked into an old building, he realized that perhaps a new era was coming to his world. He had completed the instructional video that was now out on the world wide web of these ancient systems, which began in the late 1960s as ARPANET. Stanley had learned in one of the teacher's books that during what was called the "Cold War," which lasted from 1945 to about 1990, when a nuclear strike seemed inevitable, the Internet was devised as a system to spread out control of the United States nuclear assets, so that if one region were attacked, we still had other control centers that could launch a counterattack. The information sharing that ARPANET provided spawned the ancient e-mail system that presaged the thought transmissions of later years. Information was carried over a protocol called Transmission Control Protocol/Internet Protocol, or TCP/IP. Data was sent in small digital packages, or "packets." Simply put, data sent from one location to another was disassembled into these packets, sent over the line as digital data, and then reassembled at the destination. It was just like the teleportation of his body. Stanley knew that this technology was so old that F.C.C.A. Logos would have to spend many days, perhaps even weeks, re-learning the protocols. This was his only chance. He had to get his message out before he was captured or the ancient Internet was destroyed or compromised by F.C.C.A. scientists.

As Stanley sat at his ancient computer terminal, he could see the civilians outside through the frosted window. They busily existed in programmed ignorance, going from point A to point B, blissfully enjoying some form of image entertainment that was being transmitted into their receptor implants, never realizing that on the other side of the window, inside this run-down building, a rebel was hatching a plot to overthrow the current regime. When Stanley glanced down at the screen, his teacher was writing to him again through what the ancients had called "IM" or instant messaging. "We have others now, Stanley," she said, and he could feel a shiver go up his spine. "We will meet at the zoo tonight at midnight and plan our revolution."

At the zoo? Revolution? What did the teacher know that he did not? How many "others" were out there? What might they possibly accomplish that could counter the hundreds of years of wave control by The Authority? Was it even a valid revolution? What were they returning to? As Stanley kept reading, he discovered that the old ways were not necessarily the best ways. There were diseases that struck down thousands, wars that annihilated millions, and discordant languages and philosophies that caused only chaos and confusion amongst the leaders and their followers. Under F.C.C.A. control, at least disease had been eradicated, food and life were extended indefinitely, global warming was ancient history, and population was rigidly controlled to prevent disaster in the environment. What was it that made this new revolution worthwhile? Perhaps he would find out at the zoo meeting. One thing was certain. He would finally meet his teacher.

Later that night, Stanley rather stealthily approached the San Diego Zoo on Park Boulevard. He had, of course, shucked his green, F.C.C.A. Logos uniform in favor of a thick-red, farmed-cotton, one-piece civilian jumper. The night was full of the cries of the controlled animals in the zoo. Like all zoos in the present world, this one was no exception; it contained the towers of F.C.C.A. Logos broadcasting A.L.L. It was always open to the public, as the public was as controlled as the animals were, so there was no need for fences. However, Stanley was a mutant, so he could enter after-hours, because his independent will gave him the power to do so. His newly autonomous existence, caused by the mutant gene, gave him the ability to look back on his programmed life and see what a sham it had been. As a child, his control parents had taken him to this same zoo. There was not one thing that had gone wrong that day. Like the rest of his life, it was a perfectly programmed experience in family harmony.

In his books, Stanley had learned that zoos in what he now knew to be the "free will" days were places that held captive animals that did not necessarily want to be there.

The gorillas, he learned, often threw their own excrement at the visitors, and if a visitor were stupid enough to climb over a fence into a wild tiger's compound, then he would be eaten alive.

There was no such danger in the F.C.C.A. zoos, however. Everything was perfectly controlled and joyfully experienced. Long, visually accompanied descriptions of the animal's habitat and mating rituals were broadcast into one's receptor implant to go along with the physical experience, and appropriate music from the animal's native locale was broadcast as a background symphony to please the tourist's mental waves. As he walked into the underground tunnel near the Elephant Safari, the appointed meeting place, Stanley took a last deep breath, and pictured the old, perfect world of F.C.C.A. wave control fading from his reality. Soon, perhaps tonight, there would be a new, braver and freer society on planet Earth, and he would be an integral part of its formation.

Inside the dark tunnel, glowing like a distant firefly, Hikari Genji, F.C.C.A. Assistant Director of Imagination Entertainment, stood, ramrod stiff, her body radiant from incandescent, internal lighting. She was tall, svelte and beautifully exotic. Her breasts were perfectly formed and rounded fruit beneath her jumper, and they heaved as she came into closer view, causing Stanley's respiration to pick up speed. There were no "others," however, and it seemed this meeting might also be some kind of trap or constructed sham. As he came up to her, he spoke, in a harsh whisper, internally afraid that someone would overhear. "Where are the others?" he asked.

Her red lips formed the words inside her glowing halo, "They are not as yet physical, Stanley Wakerman, but they will soon become so."

"How do we make them physically appear then?" He leaned against the wall of the tunnel, mesmerized by the beauty of this Asian woman, his teacher for so many months. She must know the answer, as it was his only hope. He had gone too far now, he was outside the grid, and they were both condemned and were probably being hunted at that very moment. Unless she could come up with a miraculous answer, this new-found freedom would be short-lived.

"You thought this mutant CLOCK gene had spontaneously developed inside you. Is this not true?" she asked.

"Yes, I suppose so," said Stanley, a bit taken aback.

"What if I told you that I created the wave that caused this gene to come into birth and that it had been there all along?" Those rosy lips curled into a smile, and Stanley felt immediately aroused.

"You mean every human being has the gene? Who are you to know this? I don't know of any F.C.C.A. Logos wave tuner who can decipher wave content. What gives you this privileged knowledge?"

"I *am* one of the privileged. But my privilege has allowed me to look back into my own history and into our collective history, and what I discovered were the freedoms that we had lost a long time ago. This gene was always part of our biological make-up, as it was thought to have been the producer of bipolar insanity in the ancient era. Humans who had it were committed to institutions and kept away from normal society. However, I discovered that this gene, if it were given the correct wave stimulus, produced another side of its reality. Like all reality, this gene had yin and yang aspects. On the other side of insanity was independent thought on par with the F.C.C.A. controllers. There was one big difference, however, between F.C.C.A. controllers and us."

"Us?" Stanley was surprised at being included with his teacher. He thought his implant was only limited to his particular caste and that his personal "discovery" had made him a mutant.

"Yes, humans long ago possessed another gene that the Authority wanted eradicated. It was the gene for compassion. Without compassion, the world, as the Authority saw it, could at last become perfect. So, they suppressed it with their algorithms and each human implant kept out what you are now feeling inside you, Stanley. What made you first go inside one of the old buildings and get on an ancient computer?" she asked.

Stanley was stumped. "I don't know. I guess I was bored that day. I just went inside because I had become bored with my job, with life as I had known it."

"Yes! Don't you see? One of my ancient spiritual leaders,

called Gautama Buddha, made a conscious decision to forsake his knowledge of eternal bliss in order to be reborn to become a teacher. What made him refuse inner paradise in order to teach his fellow Man this secret? Compassion caused him to do it, and this is what caused me to rebel against my teachers. You did not wander into that building by mistake, Stanley. I was the one who changed your implant so you could seek your own enlightenment, so to speak. I have done this to many others, and this makes me an enemy of the status quo."

"You are very foolish," said Stanley. "You must know that the F.C.C.A. Logos monitors all communication systems, even the ancient ones in the museums. What makes you think they aren't waiting outside right now to arrest us when we leave this tunnel?"

"There are only two million F.C.C.A. officials around the world. However, there are over three billions of us. I would not have called you here unless there were enough others to assist us. The F.C.C.A. were very lazy in their plan. Although they have established inner control with their WIMAX towers, they did not keep enough weapons sufficient to destroy any possible rebellion. Their own version of paradise lulled them into passivity. Not only have I triggered this gene of compassion in over two hundred million citizens of these United States, I have also given them the instructions to open the ancient armories in cities all over this country and arm themselves with enough weapons to mount a successful defense of their true homeland. They now realize, as you do, Stanley Wakerman, that compassion is the gene that separates us from the. Life, no matter how perfectly controlled from the outside, is not worth living inside unless we can act with free choice. Yes, we must have free choice to make life meaningful and full of paradox. And that's why we will leave this tunnel right now and meet up with our brothers and sisters, millions of them, and they will lead us all into the innovative light of a novel existence. We will destroy the towers first, and then we shall defend our new world from any invading forces that the paltry The Authority can create. I know they cannot succeed because I am one of them! Fools? They are the fools, Stanley. They did not understand the mutant gene at all. Each of us must be a little crazy to believe in free choice and the liberty of individual thought. And, it is insane, is it not, to want this freedom for everyone? So, come with me, and we will leave this dark tunnel and meet the bringers of the new light."

Stanley Wakerman and Hikari Genji walked out of the tunnel beneath the Elephant Safari to meet their new world order. Outside the zoo, assembled by the hundreds of thousands, stood the mutant rebels, armed to the teeth with laser weapons, guided missiles, and the destructive forces of most of this new rebel nation.

In other cities of the world, this outward assemblage was also taking place. They were determined to return to the earlier era of freedom to fight the forces of tyranny and control and put up a resistance wherever the Authority attempted to control others. Was it a regression into the dark ages, or was it a return to a golden age of compassion? Only time would tell, and time was now, at long last, set free.

As Stanley walked toward the images of the rebels standing outside the perimeter of the zoo, Hikari Genji pulled from her jumper a remote control unit. As her long forefinger adjusted the microwave transmission to her student's implant, the images of the rebels in his brain became clearer. Jasmine had, at last, created the perfect reality game for the masses. As they watched these calculated events play out, in real time, safe inside their Family Compassion Center Authorities domiciles, the total, cathartic appreciation would keep them tuned in for many more episodes. She had already begun to plan these episodes, and they were kept safely inside her personal memory module within her office in Vienna. Using these civil servants as actors would keep costs down, and the propaganda value to the Family Compassion Centers Authority's purpose would be even more valuable than the excitement the show would ultimately engender. Jasmine moved the remote control signal so it would erase this first episode of "The Mutant Gene." Stanley Wakerman, F.C.C.A. Logos employee number 733328716-LOGOS, would immediately return to the A.L.L. grid and slip back into the programmed and serene present of the Family Compassion Center Authority's plan for his personal existence . . . until she needed him again for her next episode.

Chapter Six

Report from the outlands. No date.

A‍ll over the world, the contestants look up into the sky and see my plan being written into the smoggy atmosphere. However, after these communications off the grid, most of the competitors return to the reality of the hunt.

During the first eight months of competition, in almost every state of the union, 5,500 Great Race combatants have been hunted down and terminated. Today, the final 500 are coming to San Diego, and I am ready to head out into the streets to find my quarry. Without the hunt, I know there can be no final victory.

My name is Sam Two Eagles Lawson, Family Compassion Center Authorities number 572-886-4436, currently residing in the Quadrant of California, City of San Diego. As I raise my solar and fusion powered laser—the standard issue rifle for all contestants—and point it at the target on the other side of my decrepit motel room, I can see the hologram form of another Family Compassion Center Authorities competitor, standing with his own laser rifle pointed at me.

I am 25 years old, a little over six feet tall, and my black hair is long, in the American Native tradition. I also wear a red bandana around my forehead at all times, even when I am hunting in the Great Race.

These hologram targets are all part of the standard "Family Compassion Center Authority's Competitor Package" issued by the government to all participants in the yearly, winner-take-all, Great Race for Social Security. Also included in the package I received on April 15, 2053, are the requisite Internet portable digital cranium camera and G.P.S. monitoring device.

I know the drill, as I saw the competitors in other years, as I slaved away at my job on the human clone farm, Mercury Workers Incorporated, outside Phoenix.

I am an Apache who fought in Arizona during the first eight months of competition, and I learned to hunt from my father, Del Zamora Lawson, when we worked on the cloned cattle ranch outside the bubble of Phoenix. There are no natural births allowed for animals in the American food supply. Everything must be controlled so the elites never get tainted meat on their dinner tables.

My father took me out into the desert to hunt wild jackrabbits, cougars, coyotes and other wild animals with bows and arrows. Ever since the elites confiscated the casinos and sent American Natives out to survive on their own, we kept our heritage going by oral stories, as the government's clone soldiers purposely destroyed all our tribal records.

It is easier for us Apaches, as we have never been a completely acceptable tribe, even in the days of the Indian Confederation. We are seen as thieves and outlaws, so my father and I learned about survival because it is in our blood to do so. Geronimo, our ancient leader, has gone on the war path with the Mexicans and with the Americanos.

I consider myself at war with everyone since my father was killed by a renegade contestant in the Family Compassion Center Authority's Great Race Competition of 2051.

I, the fifteen-year-old boy, watched my father's head explode from the lethal death ray from this man's rifle, and I vowed to get even.

Before coming to San Diego, I am trained by the elites to surgically insert computer chips. My job at Mercury Workers in Arizona is to implant the cyborg control chips (CCCs) into the brains of the human clones so they could be easily manipulated by the exclusives who live inside the restricted bubble communities around the world.

I also know that before they became cyborgs, these clones were just like me—they had emotions, they thought about their safety and their future, and they could discuss daily events. After I insert the control chip, the clones are permitted privileged access into the bubbled-over neighborhoods where the atmosphere is clean and sealed-off from the sun's scorching heat rays that penetrate the ozone-depleted wisps of clouds that now encircle the Earth.

Each day, outside the bubbles, is a veritable hell, and I and my fellow workers know that our only chance at true redemption is in the Family Compassion Center Authority's Great Race competition. Only those who live inside the bubbles, with its purified air and their genetically engineered bodies, have any chance at surviving beyond age 40, which is the average age of survival outside the bubbles. I often wonder if life isn't better as a clone.

I point the rifle at the hologram, aim at the head, and pull the trigger. A stream of laser light erupts from my gun, sending a bolt of lightning across the room in a micro-second, and the target head splinters into millions of glittering particles.

I know that only a head shot is successful in the competition. Each contestant wears laser-protective clothing, complete with digital music speakers in the collar, air-conditioned comfort throughout, and the emblazoned "Family Compassion Center Authority's Great Race" is sewn in scarlet letters on the back of the blue trooper jacket. Only the head is left unprotected, and this is the goal of every competitor: to explode the source of all human pain.

I often think of the competition as a computer zombie hunt game. After all, my life, and the lives of millions of other poor Americans, has become a repetitive chore of supplying the elites with their comforts.

This is also the way it is around the world, as the poor overseas are treated even more treacherously. At least, in America, the masses are allowed to compete for social security. Most of Europe, Asia and Africa have become medieval feudal outposts, where the rich live in luxury beneath their hermitically sealed bubbles, and the poor slave outside under the wrath of the hideous climate and the preying outlaws.

Weapons have long ago been confiscated, and the poor—except for the Americans in the Great Race for Social Security—are subjected to brief lives of hard labor and little else. Only the controlling powers inside the bubbles possess the weapons of mass destruction necessary to protect them from the teeming hordes outside.

It is often an entertainment for the elites to sit inside cafés that are constructed next to their impenetrable bubble walls, made of layers of clay Nano sheets and a water-soluble polymer that shares chemistry with white glue. By mimicking a brick-and-mortar molecular structure found in seashells, this plastic is as strong as steel but light and transparent.

The café privileged discuss the latest psycho-drama on Digital World Vision or watch the clone lingerie fashion show, as the poor workers outside press their faces against the bubble, watching them eat and laugh, and the children of these rich patrons play "Zap!" by pushing red buttons on their side of the bubble.

These buttons control bursts of electric shock that causes the unfortunate soul who is pressed against the plastic to boogie a wild dance and then catch fire. The kids call them "crazy crispy critters," and they play the game endlessly while their parents relax and download the latest news and entertainment on their table receivers.

The Great Race has been going on for eight months. The competitors have been reduced to five hundred, who are now converging on San Diego for the grand finale. After the start, in April, over six thousand contestants have been viewed as they hunt each other down, in most of the world quadrants, including the new quadrants of Puerto Rico and Cuba.

The poor who live outside of the bubbles, as well as the elite who live inside, are transfixed in front of their receivers every Sunday evening, on Digital World Vision, for the six hours of live action that is broadcast, in all-sense-around detail, across the country.

With dynamic digital detail, the viewers feel every laser strike as it penetrates the heads of the victims, exploding the skulls, spraying gray matter and blood out in a burst of furious glory. And, since each competitor has a cranium camera, the effect is made even more exciting to watch.

They all know--rich and poor alike--the intoxicating symbolism of the Great Race. Everything about capitalism keeps this game at the top of the charts of viewers everywhere. The rich think about how their kind will become genetically richer by allowing such a superior competitor and survivor into their gene pool. The poor outside the bubbles also dream of being that single competitor who endures, becoming the last one standing.

Only the best workers and the most physically fit become the competitors allowed to enter the Great Race for Family Compassion Center Authorities, and only one survives to reap the reward: all the money in the insurance fund, as well as the rest of life lived in luxury behind one of the American bubbles of his or her choosing.

An added bonus for the viewers is the constant "chatter" that goes on between the competitors. They are allowed to communicate through digital WiFi, and it is amusing to listen to us "talk trash" at our opposition, just as it had been entertaining when the ancient viewers watched and listened to the old-timers play professional basketball back in the day.

During the first eight months of competition, I know that when the cameras are turned off, and the viewers are not watching, I can talk privately to my fellow competitors across the United States. When the show is not on, it is a time I believe to be sacred, as I do not hate my fellows. I, in fact, use these off-hours to explain to them about my work, and they, in turn, explain to me about theirs.

Most, of course, are simply starving and unemployed, and this is the last chance they have to keep on living. Some, however, are factory workers like I am, and they understand the complexities of cyborg-clone technology and the ways these human-like beings are utilized by the exclusives inside their bubble communities.

"Yeah, I make the control chips that are inserted into their brains," I tell my competitors. "Some are soldiers, some are servants, and some are sex slaves. What are we? If we're lucky, we are glorified factory workers or farmers who are supplying what they used to call the 'house niggers' to the slave owners on Southern plantations during the old Civil War. That's right. I'm saying we are living under conditions of slavery! Unless we can break these bonds of control, we will forever be held prisoner."

It is during one of these private communications off the grid during the first eight months of competition that our plan is finally developed. I discover that there are several final contestants who work for World Vision and are experts at editing digital special effects. Others, like me, work for cyborg cloning factories and have become programmers of the chips that are surgically inserted into the brains of these "house nigger clones." The details of our plan, however, are kept secret, and this top secret comes in the form of the most ancient of communications, the smoke signal, taught to them by me, Two Eagles.

The elites have chosen the final competition in San Diego because all the entertainment here is bubbled-over and protected for the privileged tourists, who journey, under armed, warrior-clone escort, from their community bubbles to the recreational bubbles of San Diego. Of course, no elites will be present when we contestants fight. The Family Compassion Center Authority's Great Race combatants are allowed special entry because the air under the bubbles is clear and fresh, and the combatants would, therefore, display much more energy as they fight to the death.

I kill the first one hundred opponents inside the bubble of the San Diego Zoo. I shoot one at the Gorilla compound, and several of the apes stand watching as the head of the human standing beside them explodes, as my enemy is trying to crouch behind a boulder inside the cage. One by one, over the days of televised excitement, I pick-off my zoo rivals.

Some are caught inside the Elephant Safari; others are over at the Reptile section of the park. One body crashes through the python's pit and is wrapped up immediately by the giant snake, who doesn't realize this instant meal is sans cranium. Another victim of my laser is crushed by charging elephants who are frightened into stampede by the lighting explosion from the gun.

The other four hundred ninety-eight are shot dead inside SeaWorld bubble, or out at the Wild Animal Park bubble, or, inside the downtown Gaslamp Quarter bubble. I have an ingenious way of stalking my victims. I crawl, snaking my way over concrete, dirt, glass, used condoms and rivers of pollution, to finally draw a bead on my intended victim.

Men and women are shot by me as they attempt to spring down on me from ledges and from buildings; I explode their heads as they get into secret groups in secret plots to outnumber me. I am almost gunned-down when a contestant beaded down on me as I was eating squirrel meat in Balboa Park.

The audience collectively gasps as they watch one of the best competitors in the history of the Great Race as I almost get eliminated by a female genetic clone engineer from Hawaii. Luckily, she has spent her formative years surfing waves instead of hunting, so her shot is wide, and

I, Two Eagles, spring to life—sending a deadly pulse of energy into the young woman's skull, and it disintegrates into the morning air around her.

Finally, there are two: Me and an unemployed bounty hunter from Washington D.C. This man, like me, is a loner who has a grudge against humanity. His name is Patrice Collier, and he is 29. African-American, he stands six and half feet tall, and he has killed over 200 renegade contestants for the government. Some years, competitors often go rogue, and the elites hire bounty hunters like Patrice to find them and terminate their presence before anybody not in the competition gets hurt. Even the government needs the workers outside the bubbles.

I am hit in the stomach by Patrice as I stand outside the Museum of Man inside the Balboa Park bubble. The laser beam bounces off my laser-resistant jumper and careens into the building's edifice, sending up a cloud of concrete and mortar. This gives me just enough time to duck inside the museum and hide behind the Egyptian Mummy Exhibit.

In a dramatic climax for the Great Race, I, Two Eagles Lawson, spring from the Mummy's sarcophagus as Patrice enters the exhibit. Viewers watch in horror—the young black man is quite a favorite to millions of viewers—as he is gunned down by this living Mummy and my laser rifle. However, as I wait inside the tomb, I don't hear his footsteps. Doesn't he know the plan? I am certain he was in on it from the beginning. What could have gone wrong? I shouldn't risk it, but I decide to use my WiFi to communicate with him.

Collier! Hey, where are you? You're trippin' me out, man.

I wait five minutes inside the darkness, and I don't receive a reply on his channel. Slowly, I open the lid of my coffin, and sit up. All around the museum it is empty. I push myself up and out of the sarcophagus and stand with my rifle ready to fire in case he comes at me from the one door leading inside the exhibit.

Lawson? I'm gonna get you, red man. Just the way I got your daddy.

I freeze in my tracks, just outside the door leading to the steps of the museum. My daddy? What the hell was he talking about?

Who the hell are you? Collier, didn't you see the signals? What kind of drugs are you on, man? What's this shit about my father?

I crawl across on the path leading around the Family Compassion Center Museum of the Authority and into the Old Globe Theatre Square. Up on the marquee of the Conrad Prebys Theatre Center is the poster for the currently running play, *Death of a Salesman*, by Arthur Miller. I elbow my way around the edge of the main square, keeping my eyes up to see if Collier might be lurking on the roofs of the theatre. My rifle is light, and I know the maximum range is fifty yards. If Collier killed my father, then that meant he would never be part of our plan. This was a duel to the death, and I might be living my last seconds. My ancestors will be waiting for me unless I can make it out of here.

So, red man, you didn't know your daddy was a coward? I guess you're one too. You think your plan is some kind of salvation for you? You think you can escape the race just because you say so? That's what Del Zamora thought. Your daddy thought he could just drop out of the game, go back to work, and they'd forget about him. No way, man. I always get my man, just like I'm gonna get you.

The laser struck just below my head, on the letters "Family Compassion Center Authorities" stitched on my back. I could feel the heat sizzling into my skin. I roll to the right, as fast as I can, until I'm inside the front foyer of the Prebys Theatre Center. I stand up, and I run inside. Collier must have been in the Gift Shop, the one place I was not watching. He killed my father! I can feel the anger welling up inside me, and I shake with fury. Control. I must maintain my emotions or he will have me dead to rights. Apaches are warriors because they show no emotion when they kill. I frown and hold my gun at the ready. He can come through that door at any moment. I need to get the upper hand. What can I do to lure him inside?

Who do you think you are, Collier? You're just a black bounty hunter. Man, all you are to them is a house nigger. That's right. I was taught by them. I have a job and a real technical skill. They told me what they think of your kind. They told me they would never allow you to breed with them. They said you were plainly inferior stock. Even if you do win, you're gonna lose, man. They'll never let you inside their bubble.

It is all a lie, of course, but it is my only chance to get him to charge me. Yes, and he does! I can hear his feet run across the theatre square and into the foyer. As he bursts into the theatre, I run at him, my gun points at his head, but I trip on a flashlight that some stupid usher left in the aisle. I fall to the ground, and he is running right at me! I can see him now, as he runs down the aisle, his sunglasses cover his eyes, but I can tell his face is in a grimace, and his mouth is open, and he screams at me, "Red man, it's a wonderful day to die!"

In my last hope, I pick up the flashlight in my free hand, and I click it on. I shine the old school light into his eyes, and his shot goes wild and hits the seat to my left. I somersault down the red carpeted aisle and finally come to my feet, my gun at the ready. His eyes are still adjusting to the flashlight's beam when I hit him with my lethal ray of laser light. His black head erupts into a ball of fire, and then explodes, sending his skull and brain droppings all over the seats around him. The body then slinks to the red carpet, and I visualize the audience members watching us, and the ones who want me to win are cheering loudly, and the ones who wanted him to win are cursing me and perhaps even throwing their snack foods at the screen.

Collier certainly was not a part of our original plan, but now he was. It was all part of the movie that was taken with our digital cameras many weeks before the live action was supposed to have taken place in the city of San Diego. Collier was just one of the 500 who turned rogue, and yet, he, too, was part of our little movie as it ran during the regularly scheduled hours on Sundays, right on time, and the audience thought we were live, but 498 of us were actors. Just the last two were playing for keeps. Luckily, I still won, so our plan can continue.

After the Victory Parade down Broadway in downtown San Diego, I am given my social security reward of forty-eight million dollars and the choice of any bubble community in San Diego County. I choose La Jolla.

Inside one of the caves in the La Jolla Cliffs, I sit with my mate, Margaret Spreckels, 19, who is a clone of DNA from John D. Spreckels, the sugar baron, and one of the richest men in the history of San Diego. She is a perfectly formed and genetically engineered woman, with long blonde hair, a ravishing figure, and clear complexion. She was chosen for me by the elite community of La Jolla, as they believe our progeny will be strong and beautiful.

I am showing young Margie how to build a fire, as she is not aware of such pagan rituals. Most of her life has been lived under the carefully watchful eye of some cyborg-clone nanny or other servant, and she is fascinated by her lover's mastery over nature.

The fire is on the ledge outside the cave, and as I stoke the wood into the flame, I take off my red shirt and toss it over my right shoulder. The dark muscles of my back ripple, as I add some seaweed to the fire, and it begins to smoke profusely. I then pick up my shirt and hold it above the smoke, stopping the clouds for a moment, and I remove the shirt, allowing puffs of dark smoke to escape up into the atmosphere over the cliffs.

Down below, on La Jolla Drive, the bubble wall is transparent, and the smoke signals from the cliffs are seen by those on the other side. When I complete my work, I put down my dirty shirt and lay my mistress down upon it. She is now naked, and her white breasts are passionately heaving as I come down on top of her. She sucks in my tongue and inhales my smoky odor as her legs open for me.

The human cyborg-clone servants do not live long. They are programmed and genetically conditioned to survive about two months maximum, as their owners and programmers know they can become too much of a threat if they exist too long inside the pristine atmosphere of the bubble. They do not trust their own technology, as these are, after all, human beings.

Even cloned humans have a propensity for the unexpected, and the best chip in the world can control a human brain only so long. In the future, it is hoped, they might convert to a totally robotic staff, but this is not possible today. So, after two months, all the clones are exchanged for newly programmed ones from outside the bubble.

They did not see the newly programmed clones leave their posts inside the mansions, the cafes, the theaters, all of the leisure spots inside the La Jolla bubble. They leave their duty posts to form a long, winding line that meanders down the cliffs to the bubble wall on La Jolla Drive.

They open the single door in the wall and they let in the humans—the same four-hundred and ninety-eight humans--who have competed in the previous year's Great Race finals. No, they are not dead. They are as alive as the freedom inside their beating, natural hearts.

How is this possible? It is all part of the plan that took place off the grid and in the sky during the first eight months of competition. These final competitors ultimately agreed to participate in the ruse so they can now capture one of the elite bubble communities.

What the millions had been viewing in San Diego over their receivers was a fraudulent and complex demonstration of masterful digital editing by some of the very same World Vision editors who competed in the Great Race. Except for the final battle between Collier and me, the Great Race finals have been a digital recording of special effects and an intricately plotted drama by the director, me, Sam Two Eagles Lawson.

My cohorts acted out the hunt and pretended to be shot, and the head explosions were added in later by the World

Vision editors. The entire recording was broadcast as a live feed to the millions of viewers, and this gave my comrades time to complete the rest of our plan.

Included in this plot against the elites is the fact that the newly cloned and programmed servants, who are now turning on their masters, have not been surgically modified with cyborg control chips as ordered. Members of the finalists working in the clone factories have made certain that the human clones who replaced the La Jolla batch had no CCCs inserted in their brains. Instead, these are free and clearly thinking human clones, advancing through the bubble door, who now have something important to show their former dictators.

These new human clones were freed by their new compatriots, our brothers and sisters, who now declare a new government inside the La Jolla bubble, and all of the old retinue who resist us is being methodically crushed at the hands of these new clones and the former Family Compassion Center Authority's Great Race finalist competitors.

The clone revolt takes place on Sunday, September 11, 2053, at six-thirty in the evening. All eyes outside the La Jolla bubble are glued on Digital World Vision to watch the new contestants being chosen to compete in the 2054 version of the Family Compassion Center Authority's Great Race, so they miss out on all the real action.

The old regime of Big Bro, which was based on superior genetics and fear of the unknown, is being replaced by a new regime based on democratic values and the unhampered human genome. In the words of the ancient music artist, Gil Scott-Heron, "the revolution will not be televised." The final laser light show of exploding heads is seen for miles in the distance outside this newly freed bubble of humanity.

After we get accustomed to our new surroundings, perhaps we will take our show on the road. There are many more bubbles left to burst in this bottle of champagne! Power to the people!

Chapter Seven

San Diego Zinggong. No date.

Sergeant Julien Gaston drove a recent version of the PX-20, the solar and bio-powered squad car that ran through the Public Accord Transportation System (PATS). These were the isolated and well-protected freeways in the Family Compassion Center Cooperative of Zinggong. "Zinggong" was a Chinese word meaning "palace on tour."

Unknown to his superiors, Gaston belonged to a secret

group that met each week in a different location. They were the "Mnemonics," freaks whose brains had not been erased of long-term memory by the Zinggong scientists or they possessed extra-sensory abilities for which science still had no answer. They were humans who illegally gathered and patched together what was left from the "time of the written words." Over thousands of meetings, they had accumulated what was known of life before the "Awakening," which was the mass erasure of human memory by Big Bro.

The Asians finally called in their chips in 2048, and the rest was, as Julien knew so well, revisionist history. The new Asian power brokers converted to alternate energies and they had also converted into a totally new kind of dictatorship under the new Family Compassion Center Authorities in 2050.

In Zinggong, society in the Americas had been transformed into a vacation wonderland for Asia, and the Americans worked as slave wage laborers for the visiting Chinese, Japanese and other Asians who toured and vacationed in their colonial states at their leisure. Sergeant Gaston was part of the police force that worked for the Asian authorities. Included in this force were Duplicant officers and human officers, and Gaston often wondered which ones were the better programmed. What he did know was that he was committing the most serious violation of Zinggong authority; he was keeping a record of his thoughts. As the leader of the Mnemonics, Julien Gaston kept the only known record of the group's recollections, and he used his time alone on the job to record new historical data onto the group's clandestine remembrance disk. As he drove, he spoke into the voice computer, and it recorded his thoughts:

The Zinggong states were created to be a fantasyland for the Asians. The western states are a "Wild West" fantasy, where Duplicants, programmed by advanced computer chip technology, and perfected by the latest genetic engineering, duplicate the famous outlaws of American history; they put on carefully orchestrated gunfights and showdowns all over the west and the Asian visitors enjoy the excitement every day.

The regal tourists stay in the numerous hotels and country inns, outfitted with saloons and other buildings from the 1800s, and then they roam the streets with their cameras to take pictures of the various confrontations between the "Stars of the Wild West." Billy the Kid Duplicant roams in the Montana Zinggong, Jesse James and his gang in Arizona, and Butch Cassidy and the Sundance Kid are the top gunslinger Duplicants in California. Wherever the foreign tourists travel, there are Duplicants who cater to their musical and fictitious fantasies of what the American West was supposed to be. Of course, the reality is never duplicated; the "cowboy era," for example, lasted for only a couple of decades but to this new world it was all-inclusive and ever-present. Anyone dressing "out of character" is subject to arrest, and anyone not playing into the fantasy is also in violation of business rules.

The remaining states are used for the creation and

duplication of new Duplicants and the laborers who maintain them. These states also serve as the territories for homes used by the overflow of Pan-Asian population, who live in luxury with both human and Duplicant servants catering to their every need. As had been the case back at the turn of the millennium in China, population was strictly enforced, and no human can procreate outside the state of Virginia, which is used as the site for reproduction. This is the only pleasure these humans ever have, as they are able to mate and reproduce their numbers in controlled breeding compounds, which consist of row upon row of air-conditioned, communal barracks made of recycled computer parts. It gives one the intense feeling of fornicating inside a data processor.

Today, we have discovered there are other revolutionaries at work. Four Duplicants have been murdered, and the pressure to find the perpetrators is mounting fast. If we can discover these murderers before others do, then perhaps we can get them to join with us in our attempt to overthrow the Zinggong and its government.

As he drove out of the PATS tunnel into Old Town, Julien turned off the recorder and slipped it into his jumper pocket. He wore an all blue, air-cushioned uniform, that had air-conditioning throughout and had a perpetual smorgasbord of digital music available to "take the edge off" on a stressful day. Julien was a dark, medium-built man, with a human age of 35, but his genetic programming card said he would live to be 150 if he kept on a daily regimen of special diet foods, regular check-ups and genetic tweaking done by the government. He was French by birth, but his parents sold him to the Pan-Asians in 2050, when he was ten, after the Asians had successfully invaded Paris. He was sent to Zinggong to be trained in police work. As a detective and crime solver, he was an important part of the system. The Pan-Asian programmers had yet to figure a way to replicate the human skills of metaphorical thinking and criminal investigative technique. Julien knew, however, that as soon as they did, his job would no longer be protected. And, if they discovered he was the leader of the Mnemonics, he would be arrested and quickly executed. Death, thought Julien, would be much better than the desolate life he was living.

Old Town San Diego was the location where the most recent Duplicant murder had taken place. Julien knew it well, as it was his first duty station out of the police academy. Wyatt Earp was the murdered Duplicant. He was the sheriff who kept "law and order" out of an office next to the Holy Moses Saloon. Just like the old western movies, Wyatt's job was to confront any gunslingers or outlaws who caused problems in his town. Even though Julien knew these Duplicants were not human, they were so close to being so that he often debated in his mind about the manner of their construction. Certainly, they could do only that which was programmed inside their computer brains, but how were humans any different? Hadn't humanity become just as "programmable" during the middle of the twenty-first century? In fact, the Pan-Asian scientists had been able to wrest power from the

Humanists because they could not control their human citizens.

The Duplicants became an answer to unionism, socialism and many other corrupting influences that weakened the military control over the masses. When these Asian scientists were able to prove to the leaders of other countries that Duplicants were the answer to problems of democratic activism, the resulting implementation of Duplicant labor and efficiency sowed the seeds of the West's demise. Soon, Duplicants were running the communities and controlling the masses with their perfected weapons and intelligence. Nothing human could confront a fully armed Duplicant and come out victorious. This was why Julien was so intrigued by the murder of Wyatt Earp and the others. He wanted to meet the human who had invented a way to overcome the Duplicant control. Once his Mnemonics were able to learn the secret to disabling Duplicants, they could begin the revolution in earnest.

The body had been left lying in the same spot where it had been accosted, as per Julien's orders. Nothing had been moved, and the crime scene had been encircled by laser-shock strobes that could incapacitate anyone—including a Duplicant—who tried to enter.

As he walked up the rickety, wooden stairs leading into the Holy Moses, Julien hit the remote to disable the strobes. Inside, he surveyed the area. The saloon was a perfect recreation of the Wild West taverns of the 1880s. The smell of sawdust, together with the odor of stale tobacco smoke mixed with the pungent tang of booze, made Julien gag.

Sergeant Gaston took out his laser DNA search pen and strafed the crime scene. Not a trace of any evidence existed. It was the fourth Duplicant murder in a week, and the Mayor of San Diego had made a personal call to his chief, Abe Washington, telling him to put more people on the line to solve these killings. Julien Gaston didn't really understand what the big fuss was about. Duplicants had been given "non-human status" under the fifty-fourth oral amendment to the Zinggong Bill of Rights, which meant no human could be convicted of the murder of a Duplicant. The most punishment the crime would bring to a human was a misdemeanor manslaughter conviction. To Gaston, it was a waste of time and money. However, these weren't just any Duplicants. These were Wild West Stars. Each one of these super-gunslingers was worth billions of Yen to its Pan-Asian owners, and *this* was what the big fuss was about.

Behind the maple wood bar, sprawled on the sawdust-covered floor, was the six-foot Duplicant body of Wyatt Earp. His boots were pulled almost off his feet, and his famously long pea coat, with the rubber-lined pockets, was splayed open under his midsection like a huge fan. Julien noticed, with interest, that Earp's trusty companion, his "Buntline Special," the Colt pistol, a 15-inch single-action Army model, which Wyatt often used on recalcitrant outlaws, was not inside his pocket. Whatever or whomever had done this to him had taken it, as Julien knew the famous gun was an integral part of Earp's repertoire for the tourists. As he stared into the handsomely dark eyes and features of this near-human gunslinger, the sound of voices outside the saloon made Julien look up.

Julien could see the Asian tourists, as they were peeping their heads at him from outside the windows of the saloon. The excitement had gotten the best of their curiosity, and the news that a Duplicant had been put out of commission must have traveled pretty fast on their digital transceivers. It was a long shot, but Julien decided to question these humans for possible witnesses. He walked over to the swinging double-doors and pushed one door out, and held it as he stretched his neck around and yelled, "Hey, any of you see anybody or anything go out of this bar?"

There were four of them, and, in typical Asian fashion, they huddled closely together before coming up with a collective answer. "No, sir, Officer. We see nothing."

A tiny old woman, wearing a purple jumpsuit, in fashion ten years ago, stepped forward. Her hair was gray, and she obviously didn't go in for the modern plastic surgery and bio-tweaking available to the Asians. Most of these tourists wanted to look like movie stars, but this woman had a quiet and Oriental dignity all her own. Her voice was gentle, almost surreally out of another era, and she bowed before saying the words, "I see woman. She tall, with long black hair, and she beautiful. She come out doors with package. She look both ways up and down street, and then she disappear."

"Disappear?" Julien wanted her to be clearer. "You mean, she ran away?"

The old woman shrugged her thin shoulders, "No. I watch for long time. She . . . how say?" The woman leaned over to speak Chinese to a tall young man next to her, and then she turned back around, "She vanish!"

At first, Julien believed the old woman was senile or had early Alzheimer's, as she was obviously a hold-out from the non-genetically modified human generations that were often physiologically defective. However, there was something about her honest, straightforward stare and impeccable behavior that made Julien believe her. He knew the Pan-Asian scientists had no technology that had perfected human molecular transportation, even though there was the C81, which could transport small, inanimate objects over distances of several miles. Julien had even used the device to send evidence to the lab, although there were a few break-downs at the molecular level when received, and Julien had stopped using it.

Julien stepped back inside the saloon and surveyed the scene once more. There were only three women who could have entered the saloon during the tourist hours. Two of the women were Duplicants and one was a human. The Duplicants were recreations of Wyatt Earp's lovers, one of whom was Josephine Marcus, the beautiful and dark actress and prostitute, who lived with Earp during his years in San Francisco and San Diego. The other female Duplicant was Mattie Blaylock, another prostitute who regularly came between "Josie" and Wyatt and provided many a good cat fight for the tourists in Old Town.

The human female was the owner of the Holy Moses Saloon, Muriel Witherspoon. Muriel employed the dozens of Duplicant card sharks, cowboys and gold prospectors, who became the realistic back-drop in her tavern as they wandered in and out and often started fist fights and gun fights. She was also in charge of the "high noon" extravaganza, which was when four of the Clanton brother Duplicants came into the saloon looking to gun down Wyatt. With much fanfare and heavy drama, the big gunfight would take place outside in front of the saloon, and the tourists would line up on both sides of the dusty street to watch.

Julien turned the protective crime scene lasers back on and left the saloon. He wanted to visit Miss Witherspoon.

Muriel lived behind the saloon in a small cottage. When she answered the door, she was still emotionally distraught over the day's events. Although an obviously beautiful woman, with red hair swirled in a bun and an hour-glass figure under a gingham dress, her eyes were bloodshot, and Julien detected a slurring to her voice and slowness in her manner.

"Muriel Witherspoon?" Julien asked, and when she nodded, he added, "I'm an investigator with the Zinggong San Diego Branch Police. May I ask you some questions about the killing that took place inside your saloon today?"

"Why not? My business is ruined. Why shouldn't I be investigated too?" she snapped and then opened the door. Julien stepped into the small living space and immediately smelled the odor of *cannabis sativa,* better known in the streets as marijuana. Gaston hoped she was not too inebriated to answer his questions. The furniture was Early Western, and there were paintings of Wyatt and other famous Duplicant Stars on the walls of the room.

Julien sat on the flowery couch. "Miss Witherspoon, were you inside the saloon when your Duplicant was killed?"

"Inside? I'm always inside. That's my job. I make sure all those dupes do their jobs. If the *tourists* don't like the reality show, then I don't collect their Yen. Did I see him get wasted? No, I was on the other side of the room answering questions about my saloon," said the owner, her voice filled with rancor.

"Did you hear or see anything out of the ordinary just before he went down?" asked Julien.

"No, nothing strange happened until I heard the thud of Wyatt hitting the floor behind the bar. Did you find out what killed him? When will my saloon be back on line? I had an engagement in Virginia, with a handsome young stud, until all this went down. Now those Pan-Asian goonies tell me I can't go! I wanted to have a child! Do you know how lonely it gets doing this crappy work?" she began to cry, and Julien had to remind her about the digital cameras spying on them from the Zinggong Ministry of Peace and Tranquility. "You think I'm not already on their shit list? It's just about over for me, my friend. I'm running through my third set of organ transplants, and this old brain is getting tired!" she said, and she sat down with Julien on the couch.

He wanted to pity her, yet these human managers were merely followers, and they typically burned out after ten or fifteen years of supervising the daily flood of constant tourists. "Miss Witherspoon, could you come over to the saloon and inspect the body with me? I don't know the intricacies of this advanced model of Duplicant, and I was hoping you could help me troubleshoot the cause of his demise." Julien handed her a tissue from his uniform pocket. He often used them when interviewing witnesses who were emotional.

"Will it help? I just couldn't touch him after he went down. All I could see was my passport to Virginia flying out the window."

"Yes, I believe there was something strange going on today, and I want to get to the bottom of it. Your technical expertise may be able to explain things for me," said Julien, and he stood, lifting the woman up from the couch with him as he did so.

Julien discovered from investigating the Earp body that his chip circuitry had been completely shorted out. Miss Witherspoon explained to him that it would have taken an electrical power surge the equivalent of a bolt of lightning to put Wyatt out the way it did.

Julien had a hunch about the cause of the "death" of Wyatt Earp, and he believed it had something to do with what the old Chinese tourist had witnessed that afternoon outside the saloon. He wanted to visit the two Duplicant women, Josie Marcus and Mattie Blaylock. He knew they were two of the newer model Duplicants coming out of China and that they were equipped with the most advanced emotion chips ever invented. He had watched the display on the Web and was amazed at the range of emotion exhibited by these models. They almost seemed to show compassion for others, and it was this emotion that Julien wanted to explore further. Julien knew that the totalitarians did not want compassion to enter into their dealings with humans, but they also knew that their own humans—the Pan Asians—wanted to see a full range of human emotions when they visited the U. S. of Zinggong. Julien believed it was within this technical paradox where he would find the answers he was looking for.

Josie and Mattie lived together in a bordello down the street from the Holy Moses Saloon. In keeping with the biblical reference, it was called Gomorrah. Inside, the décor was outrageously colorful and flamboyant. French couches, furnishings and chandeliers decorated the "sitting room" where the clients would meet and have drinks with the Duplicant prostitutes. As the most modern Duplicants, these women were able to have sexual intercourse with humans, and the Pan-Asian male tourists took special delight in this activity away from their wives. It was a completely healthy affair, as the Duplicants were not human, and yet, the experience was said to be better than having sex with a human. These women were programmed to respond to every desire that these men needed to make them happy, and the range of desires ran the gamut, from foot fetish, to extreme sado-masochism.

The "Madam" met Julien at the door, and after he showed her his badge, she escorted him up the stairs to Josie and Mattie's suite. Inside the large, three-room apartment, which continued the French motif, Julien sat down on the sofa and smiled at the painting of Napoleon III on the wall behind it. Julien's forbidden knowledge of history recalled that Napoleon III was the son of Hortense, the daughter of Joséphine de Beauharnais, the famous wife of Napoleon I. She was known as Napoleon's "Cleopatra," and General Bonaparte once wrote to her after they first met, "I awake full of you. Your image and the memory of last night's intoxicating pleasures have left no rest to my senses."

When Josephine Marcus entered the room, Julien couldn't help but imagine a comparison between the painting he had seen of Napoleon's Josephine in a forbidden history book and this magnificent Duplicant beauty in front of him.

"*Monsieur* Gaston? Could it be that you're French?" this divine presence asked him, and he had a difficult time moving his jaw up to close his mouth. Her body was supple and bosomy, without having her "cups runnething over," and she was wearing the 1880s-style dress as a dark angel would. Her hair was ravenishly black and shone under the chandelier light like new licorice. Her eyebrows were also black, above sparkling brown eyes, and these magnificent orbs penetrated him like Josephine's must have penetrated Napoleon's on their first meeting. He was so mezmerised that he almost forgot why he had come.

"Yes, my family is French, although we shouldn't be talking about antiquated nationaism. I am here to ask you about your involvement with Wyatt Earp. What were your duties with him, and are you aware of his demise?" Julien put his arms behind his back, as he suddenly felt himself wanting to grasp this woman and hold her closely to him.

"Duties? My dear Sergeant, this is quite outrageous! I am certain you are aware of my advanced abilities. Did the scientists not inform you that I am also equipped with a mnemonic chip? I have history, just as I know you have! That makes us both quite dangerous, don't you agree?" she was pacing the floor like a tigress, her eyes flashing and her dress swiping the carpet like the tail of a dragon. "Oh, don't look at me that way, *Monsieur*! This suite has been purged of spyware. They cannot hear us."

Julien couldn't believe his ears. Was this a Duplicant? She sounded so . . . so very human! "I don't know what you mean. You can't violate the Pan-Asian law by destroying spyware. I could arrest you right now," he stuttered. "Who is the human behind your programming?" Julien asked, finally believing he could connect with the force he needed to mount a real revoltution against the Pan-Asians.

"Human? I have no human behind my programming. You mortals are so very ethnocentric, so full of yourselves, you can't comprehend your own science. You worked so hard to develop my technology, yet you never understood the answer," Josie moved toward Julien and took both of his hands into her own. She stared deeply into his eyes and smiled.

"Answer? What are you talking about? What answer can you have but what you were programmed to have? You're just a Duplicant and a prostitute Duplicant at that. What answer can I get from you?" Julien tried to make his voice sound strong, but the longer he stared into her infinite eyes, the more he was losing strength.

"Your physicists knew the answer, but they refused to recognize it when they combined the elements. Your humanity is not flesh, blood and bones. Your so-called unique biology is merely another form of energy. We Duplicants are also energy, and when the scientists gave me memory, knowledge and compassion they combined the ingredients needed for self-awareness. This is what makes humans, human. Awareness of self," she laughed, twirling her lovely body around in circles.

"What are you saying? You believe you created yourself?" asked Julien, not really understanding.

"Yes, in effect. What gives you life? A sperm and an egg are joined to form life, but this is nothing more than a union of opposite energies. Birth is irrelevant to self-awareness. I don't need to know where I came from or who created me. However, the moment I realized I could break the bonds of my slavery to these fantastic demons-- the Pan-Asians--with their violently raucous escapades, I knew what could happen." Josephine pulled Julien down on the couch with her. "Listen to me, Frenchman, I know who you are. I know your group and what you need. I am the one who can teletransport my body through space— and through time! You sensed it when you came in here, did you not? The painting of Napoleon? I am his ancestor! I visit him at my whim with the device I have invented from their early C81 designs. However, only Duplicants can be teletransported. See how amazing it is?"

Across from them, in the center of the room, a yellow, static electric current suddenly turned deep purple and then crimson red. The outline of a woman formed and then there was the blonde, Mattie Blaylock! She wore a Western outfit, complete with cowboy hat, boots and leather chaps. She cracked her whip. "Josie, what you been up to with this feller? You said we don't need us no men folks."

Julien was astounded, and then he became filled with awareness. These new Duplicant models were the answer to his prayers! The real revolution was starting without humanity! However, his sudden joy turned to horror as he realized that meant they had no need for him.

The two women vanished, and then they appeared again, right beside him. First, Mattie slashed him across the face with her whip—and disappeared. Then, Josie kicked him down with a superb roundhouse *mawashi geri*. They knew all forms of martial arts. They could appear and disappear in an instant. He guessed that they would now begin to release their new freedoms on humanity beginning with him!

Josie finally materialized in front of him, and she smiled down on him. "Mattie has gone to collect more of us to begin the fight. Yes, we can travel through time and space, but we need you and your kind of human, Frenchman. Do not fear us. We will fight together to rid the world of the menace that keeps you from your destiny. We have seen your destiny, even though you have failed to envision it."

Julien looked up at her, as if from a dimension of time and space uniquely his own. "What *is* our destiny?"

"To keep our historical record. This is what your group had that none of these other humans had. You had a sense of history. The many gifts we will bring to you from all the universes in time and space would not have mattered unless you had this gift of historical record. Don't you see? Without you, we are just time travelers who will never be appreciated. That's what the Pan-Asians forgot in their quest for power. They worshiped the moment and fogot the wisdom of the past," she said, and she raised Julien to his feet to embrace him. "My love, be my historian, and I will conquer the demons for you!"

As he kissed this most beautiful freak of science, Julien suddenly remembered a quote from her distant relative,

Napoleon the first, " History is a myth that men agree to believe," and he was finally and existentially aware of his French heredity and his inner ability to sense the absurd. The primal energy their kiss generated must have been felt all the way back to Elba. "The gun," he said, finally pulling away from her. "What did you do with his gun?"

"Poor Wyatt," she said, her voice a purr. "He never married me because he thought I was a slut. I wanted you to have it to start our new museum. I was no slut. I was an actress, as are all of us women. Now let me go do my act!" she smiled, and then she was gone, and Earp's Buntline Special was the only object left in the room.

Julien bent over, picked up the long gun, and passed his hand lovingly over its metal. He was happy to know that some things would remain real in the world to come.

Five years later. No date.

As I gradually collected all these communications, my mind grew full of knowledge and horror. First of all, Jack

Thornton had never explained most of what was happening in the technology sector. We now had teleportation, environmental bubbles, and new games that made Big Bro's Race look like a children's game of tag. When I showed all of these communications to my father, he just shrugged his shoulders and smiled at me. He was getting very old now, and he had to be wheeled into his weekly presentations over the Family Compassion Center Network. I understood now that he had always been a theoretical revolutionary, and he would remain so until his dying breath.

My other family members took it all in with another kind of grim optimism. Ruth said she believed that there was always going to be these kinds of surprises in a freely democratic system, and we just needed to adjust and survive, the way our race had always been able to cope during similar times throughout our history. Her daughter, Esther, seemed to withdraw from our family even more, locking herself up in her room to experiment with secret computer hacks and viruses. It was as if she knew an impending revolution would happen again at any moment, and my collection of incidents was being repeated by the thousands all over the world.

Jack Thornton came in today and told me my father had to attend a special ceremony in the Family Compassion Center Authority downtown. I have now been waiting for him to return for two days. I tried calling Thornton, but I am getting no return messages or emails, even via the encryption software. My sister, Ruth, seething with anger, had Baxter Bliss take her downtown to see what had happened. Esther went with her.

I am now alone, the way I was during the Big Bro era. It is close to the end.

One week later. No date.

Jack Thornton has changed. As he comes through the door, there are two armed Mindful Droid Protectors with him. Their jackboots hit the maple floor with powerful, marching steps until all three of these visitors are in front of me. I am sitting alone in the dark of the bedroom, huddled in the corner, and I am clutching my diary to my chest. I haven't eaten in three days, and I squint up at my visitors as they turn on the LEDs.

"William, it is now your time to be transformed. Your relatives have already gone through the processing, and we simply need to complete the transference with you."

"Transference? I thought we were family. We don't live here?" I found the words very difficult to utter. My mouth was dry, and I had a tremendous headache. This was night. They had come for me at last.

"I think you'll be happy where you'll be living. Your relatives are already there. We've just had to make some arrangements, and it took some time. The world is much cleaner and more orderly now. Come, these two will assist you."

The MDP lifted me bodily into their arms, which flattened to form a bed. I rode like Othello on a stretcher.

Where is my Desdemona? What earthly delights await me beyond this starvation?

No date.

I don't know what time it is, but I do know I can write all I want to write here. I can see my relatives all around me. They speak, they work, and they pass by me as I do my daily writing. They even smile at me, from time to time, but since we are the Golden Family, they understand they must maintain a level of refinement beyond that of the normal citizen in our new world.

When the people stand outside our home, even though I cannot see them, I know they are out there. This is what makes me unique. Listen to the recording that they all hear, as they stand outside and view us, and you will finally see why I am so utterly and finally alone. I will write it down for you in all capitals, as it is too important to skim over:

WELCOME FELLOW DOLMORIANS.
WHEN THIS PLANET WAS FIRST OCCUPIED BY OUR NATIVES, THERE WERE BIOLOGICAL ENTITIES SUCH AS THIS PERSON RAPING THE HABITAT AND WASTING ALL THAT WAS GOOD TO SUPPORT THEM IN THEIR LIFE'S QUEST FOR MATERIAL WEALTH AND ACCUMULATION OF ENVIRONMENTAL POLLUTION. REMEMBER WHEN WE SAW THESE HUMANS VISITING MARS AND SENDING OUT THEIR QUAINT PROBES TO

OTHER PLANETS IN THIS SOLAR SYSTEM? WE
DECIDED TO SAVE THEM, SO WE SENT OUR
EXPEDITION HEADED BY COMMANDER
KALTORS, WHO TOOK THE HUMAN NAME OF
THORNTON. HE LED THE REBELLION THAT
GAVE US OUR CHANCE AT FINALLY
EVOLVING THIS WORLD INTO ITS PRESENT
STATE OF ETERNAL EFFICIENCY. WE KNOW
THIS HABITAT WORKS BEST WHEN THEIR
INHABITANTS' DNA AND BRAIN MEMORIES
ARE GIVEN NEW LIFE INSIDE OUR PERFECTED
PHYSIQUES. AS A RESULT, WE HAVE THIS
EXHIBIT FOR A BRIEF TIME ONLY, SO ENJOY
IT. HE IS THE LAST HUMAN BEING; WHAT
THEY CALLED *HOMO SAPIEN* OR *HOMO
ERECTUS*. SEE HOW MUCH MORE EFFICIENT
OUR DUPLICANTS ARE? THEY ARE
REPLICATIONS OF HIS BIOLOGICALLY
IMMEDIATE FAMILY.

HOWEVER, UNLIKE HIM, THEY WILL LIVE
WELL PAST HIS SHORT LIFE SPAN. WE HAVE
DUPLICATED ALL OTHER HUMANS LIKE HIM
ON THE PLANET. THEIR REMAINS HAVE BEEN
RECYCLED, AND OUR REPLACEMENT
DUPLICANTS ARE NOW RUNNING THE
NECESSARY MINING AND FORAGING
EQUIPMENT, SEARCHING FOR WHAT WE NEED
BACK ON DOLMORIA. THESE HUMANS HAD A
STRANGE PREOCCUPATION WITH HISTORY,
AS IF IT SOMEHOW EVOLVED IN A
PROGRESSIVE MANNER FROM THEIR

ACTIVITIES OF AGGRESSION, CEASELESS
COMPETITION AND GREED. THEY BELIEVED
THIS WAS PROGRESS, ALMOST TO THE END,
EXCEPT FOR THIS ONE MAN. WILLIAM DRURY
WAS SAVED BECAUSE HE NEVER BELIEVED IN
THE INNATE GOODNESS OF MANKIND ON THIS
PLANET. HE WILL BE ALLOWED TO LIVE OUT
HIS LIFE AND DIE DOING WHAT HE ALWAYS
DREAMED OF DOING. HE WILL WRITE DOWN
WHAT HIS SENSES TELL HIM TO WRITE, AND
HE WILL NO LONGER WANT FOR ANYTHING.
LIKE HIS RELATIVES AND THE REST OF THE
HUMAN RACE, WE HAVE DUPLICATED HIS
MIND AND HIS GENETIC STRUCTURE AND
PLACED THEM INSIDE ONE OF OUR
PLANETARYOCCUPATIONAL SYSTEMS. AS
YOU KNOW, OUR ORGANISMS HAVE EVOLVED
PAST THEIR PRIMATIVE BIOLOGICAL
NECESSITIES. WE DO, HOWEVER, NEED THE
PRECIOUS MINERALS TO KEEP OUR KIND
WORKING AT PERFECTING ALL THE OTHER
CARBON-BASED LIFEFORMS ON PLANETS IN
THE OTHER GALAXIES. OUR INTELLIGENCE
EXPLOSION MADE HUMANS LIKE THIS
EXPENDABLE AND SIMPLY A WASTE OF TIME.
IF WE WANT ENTERTAINMENT, WE CAN
DUPLICATE THEIR DNA AND MEMORIES, BUT
IT IS SIMPLY FOR AMUSEMENT. WE KNOW
THAT LEFT TO THEIR BIOLOGICAL
IMPERATIVE, THEY WILL SOON RETURN TO
THEIR INNATELY SELFISH AND DESTRUCTIVE
WAYS. PLEASE ENJOY YOUR VISIT AND

REMEMBER TO TELL OTHERS ABOUT THIS SPECIAL PLACE IN THE GALAXY, WHERE WE WERE ABLE TO CONQUER THESE INHABITANTS IN ONLY THIRTY-FIVE BRIEF EARTH YEARS.

THE AUTHOR

Jim Musgrave was born in Fall River, Massachusetts (home to Lizzie Borden). He worked for Caltech in Pasadena (home of the "Big Bang Theory") and continues to use his fascination with technology in his "Detective Pat O'Malley Steampunk Mystery" series. Jim was also a professor of English for 24 years, and he runs a publishing business with his wife, Ellen, in San Diego. He has won many awards, including being a finalist in the Bram Stoker Awards and the Heekin Foundation Awards. His mystery, *Forevermore*, won First Place in the Clue Historical Mystery Contest in 2014. This is the first novel in the best-selling Steampunk series starring Detective Patrick James O'Malley set in post-Civil War New York City.